CONVENIENTLY WED TO THE GREEK

BY

KANDY SHEPHERD

MILLS
BOON

First published in Great Britain 2017
By Mills & Boon, an imprint of HarperCollins*Publishers*
1 London Bridge Street, London, SE1 9GF

Large Print edition 2017

© 2017 Kandy Shepherd

ISBN: 978-0-263-07138-2

Our policy is to use papers that are natural, renewable and recyclable products and made from wood grown in sustainable forests. The logging and manufacturing processes conform to the legal environmental regulations of the country of origin.

Printed and bound in Great Britain
by CPI Antony Rowe, Chippenham, Wiltshire

To Catherine and Keith,
with thanks for introducing me
to the beauty of the Ionian Islands.

CHAPTER ONE

ADELE HUDSON WAS too busy concentrating on the yoga teacher's instructions to take much notice of the latecomer who took a place to her left and unrolled his mat. From the corner of her eye she registered that he was tall, black-haired, and with the lean, athletic body she would expect from a man who did yoga. *Nice.* But that was as far as her interest went.

Until she attempted to balance on one leg, with the other tucked up against her upper inner thigh, in the *vrksasana* or 'tree' pose. It seemed impossible for a beginner. Why had she thought this class was a good idea?

Dell risked a glance to see if the guy next to her was doing any better. He held the pose effortlessly, broad shoulders, narrow hips, tanned muscular arms in perfect alignment. But the shock of recognition as he came into focus made her wobble so badly she had to flail her arms to stay upright.

Alexios Mikhalis. It couldn't be him. Not here in this far-flung spa retreat on the south coast of New South Wales where she had come to find peace. Not now when she so desperately needed to regroup and rethink her suddenly turned upside down life. But a second quick glimpse confirmed his identity, although he looked very different from the last time she had seen him three years ago pummelling her reputation in court. This man had done everything in his power to destroy her career. And very nearly succeeded.

A shiver of dread ran through her—threatening her balance in more ways than one. He was the last person on earth she wanted to encounter. She had more than enough on her mind without having to shore up her defences against him. Quickly Dell looked away, praying her nemesis hadn't recognised her. Tragedy had visited him since they'd last met, but she doubted he would be any less ruthless. Not when it came to her.

'Lengthen up through the crown of your head,' the yoga teacher intoned in her breathy Zen-like voice.

But it was no use. Dell's concentration was shot. *Why was he here?* The more she tried to balance on one shaky leg, the more impossible the pose seemed. How the heck did you lengthen through the crown of your head anyway? In spite of all efforts to stay upright, she tilted sideward, heading for a humiliating yoga wipe-out.

A strong, masculine hand gripped her elbow to steady her. *Him.* 'Whoa there,' came the deep voice others might find attractive but she had only found intimidating and arrogant.

'Th…thank you,' she said, her chin down and her eyes anywhere but at him, pretending to be invisible. But to no avail.

His grip on her arm tightened. *'You,'* he said, drawing out the word so it sounded like an insult.

Dell turned her head to meet his hawk-like

glare, those eyes so dark they were nearly black. She tilted her chin upwards and tried without success to keep the quiver from her voice. 'Yes, *me*.'

Her final encounter with him burned in her memory. Outside the courthouse he had stood on the step above her using his superior height to underline the threat in his words. *'The judge might have ruled in your favour but you won't get away with this. I'll make sure of that.'*

In spite of his loss since then, she had no doubt he still meant every word.

'What are you doing here?' His famously handsome face contorted into a frown.

'Apart from attempting to learn yoga?' she asked with the nervous laugh that insisted on popping out when she felt under pressure. 'Resting, relaxing, those things you do when you come to a health spa.' She didn't dare add *reviewing this new resort*.

This was the tycoon hotelier who had chosen to do battle with her. She was the food critic who had dared to publish a critical review of the most established restaurant in his empire. He'd sued the newspaper that had employed her for an insane amount of money and lost.

Alex Mikhalis had not liked losing. That he was a winner was part of the ethos he'd built up around him—the hospitality mogul who launched nightclubs and restaurants that instantly became Sydney's go-to venues, wiped out his competitors and made him multiple millions. '*Playboy Tycoon with the Magic Touch*'— her own newspaper had headlined a profile on him not long before her disputed review.

After the scene on the courtroom steps, she'd been careful to stay out of his way. Then he'd disappeared from the social scene that had been his playground. Even the most intrepid of her journalist colleagues hadn't been able to find him. *And here he was.*

'You've hunted me down,' he said.

'I did no such thing,' she said. 'Why would I—?'

'Please, *silence*.' The yoga instructor's tone was now not so Zen-like.

'Let's take this outside,' he said in a deep undertone, maintaining his grip on her elbow.

Dell would have liked to shake off his hand, then place her hands on his chest and shove him away from her. But she was a guest at the spa—here at the owner's invitation—and she didn't want to cause any kind of disruption.

'Sorry,' she mouthed to the instructor as she let herself be led out of the room, grateful in a way not to have to try any more of those ridiculously difficult poses.

With the door to the yoga room shut behind them, Dell took the lead to one of the small guest lounges scattered through the resort. Simple white leather chairs were grouped around a low table. It faced full-length glass windows that looked east to a view of the Pacific Ocean, dazzling blue in the autumn morning sun filtered through graceful Australian eucalypts.

Now she did shake off his arm. 'What was that all about?'

'My right to privacy,' he said, tight-lipped.

Dell was struck again by how different the

tycoon looked. No wonder she hadn't immediately recognised him. Back then he'd been a
style leader, designer clothes, a fashionable short
beard, hair tied into a man bun—though not in
court—flamboyant in an intensely masculine
way. She'd often wondered what his image had
masked. Now he was more boot camp than boutique—strong jaw clean shaven, thick dark hair
cropped short, pumped muscles emphasised by
grey sweat pants and a white singlet. Stripped
bare. And even more compelling. Just her type
in fact—if he had been anyone but him.

'And I impinged on your privacy how?' she
asked. 'By taking a yoga class that you happened
to join? I had no idea you were here.'

'Your newspaper sent you to track me down.'
It was a statement, not a question.

'No. It didn't.' The fact she no longer worked
for the paper was none of his concern. 'I'm a
food writer, not an investigative journalist.'

His mouth twisted. 'Does that matter? To the
media I make good copy. No matter how hard
I've worked to keep off the radar since…since…'

He seemed unable to choke out the words. She noticed tight lines around his mouth, a few silver hairs in the dark black of his hair near his temples. He was thirty-two, three years older than her, yet there was something immeasurably weary etched on his face.

Another shiver ran up Dell's spine. How did she deal with this? This wealthy, powerful man had been her adversary. *He had threatened her with revenge.* She was convinced his attack on her newspaper had led in part to her losing her job. But how could she hold a grudge after what he had endured?

'I know,' she said, aware her words were completely inadequate. Just a few months after his unsuccessful court case against her, his fiancée had been taken hostage by a crazed gunman in one of his city restaurants. She hadn't come out alive. His grief, his anger, his pain had been front-page news. Until he had disappeared.

Wordlessly, he nodded.

'I'm so sorry,' she said. 'I…wanted to let you know that when…when it happened. But we weren't exactly friends. So I didn't. I've always regretted it.'

He made some inarticulate sound and brushed her words away. But she was glad she had finally been able to express her condolences.

She was surprised at the rush of compassion she felt for him at the bleak emptiness of his expression. *He had lost everything.* She didn't know where he had been, why he was back. His colourful and tragic history made him eminently newsworthy. But she wouldn't make a scoop of his secret by selling the story of her encounter with him. In spite of the fact such a story would bring her much-needed dollars.

'Be assured I won't be the one to reveal your whereabouts,' she said. 'Not to my press contacts. Not on my blog. I'm here for the rest of the week. I'll stay right out of your way.'

She left him looking moodily out to the waters of Big Ray beach and had to slow her pace to something less than a scurry. No way did she want this man to think she was running away from him.

* * *

In theory, Alex should not have seen Adele Hudson again. The Bay Breeze spa was designed for tranquil contemplation as well as holistic treatments. In the resort's airy white spaces there was room for personal space and privacy.

But only hours after the yoga class he encountered her in the guest lounge, still in her yoga pants and tank top, contemplating the range of herbal teas and chatting animatedly to an older grey-haired woman who was doing the same. He was on the hunt for caffeine so did not back away. Not that he was in the habit of backing away. He'd always thrived on confrontation.

Alex had always regarded the sassy food critic as an adversary—an enemy, even. Back then he had been implacable in protecting every aspect of his business—an attack on it was an attack on *him*. He certainly hadn't registered anything physical about the person he'd seen as intent on undermining his success with her viperish review of his flagship restaurant. Yet now, observing her, he was forced to concede she was an attractive woman. Very attractive. And in spite of their past vendetta, he had seen compassion and understanding in her eyes. Not the pity he loathed.

She wasn't anything like the type of woman he'd used to date—blonde and willowy models or television celebrities who'd looked good on his arm for publicity purposes. Mia had been tall and blonde too. He swallowed hard against the wave of regret and recrimination that hit him as it always did when he thought about his late fiancée and forced himself to focus on the present.

Adele was average height, curvier than any model, with thick auburn hair she'd worn tied back in the yoga class but which now tumbled around her shoulders. She wasn't conventionally pretty—her mouth was too wide, her jaw line rather too assertive for 'pretty'—but she was head-turning in her own, vibrant way. It was her smile he was noticing now—she'd never had cause to smile in his presence. In fact he remembered she'd been rather effective with a snarl when it had come to interacting with him.

Her mouth was wide and generous and she had perfect teeth. When she laughed at something the other woman said her whole face lit up; her eyes laughed too. What colour were they? Green? Hazel? Somewhere in between? The other woman was charmed by that smile. Alex could tell that from where he stood.

Yet when Adele looked up and caught him observing her the smile faded and her face set in cool, polite lines. Her shoulders hunched as if to protect herself from him and her eyes darted past him and to the doorway. Who could blame her for her dislike of him? He wished he could make up to her for the way he'd behaved towards her. As he'd tried to make amends to others he'd damaged by his ruthless, self-centred pursuit of success. Make amends to them because he could never make amends to Mia. Her death hung heavily on his conscience. *His fault.*

He headed towards Adele. She smiled at him. But it was a poor, forced shadow of the smile he'd seen dazzling her companion just seconds before—more a polite stretching of her lips. He found himself wanting to be warmed by the real deal. But not only did he not deserve it from this person he had so relentlessly hounded, it would be pointless.

There was something frozen inside his soul that even the most heartfelt of smiles from a lovely woman could never melt. Something that had started to shut down the day he'd got a phone call from the police to say a psycho had his city restaurant in lockdown and was holding his fiancée hostage with a gun to her head. Something that had formed cold and rock solid when Mia had lost her own life trying to save another's.

'Hello there,' Dell said very politely. Then turned to the woman beside her and gestured towards him. 'We met in the yoga class,' she explained, not mentioning his name by way of introduction.

So she intended to keep her word about maintaining his privacy. He was grateful for that. Alex nodded to the older woman. He did not feel obliged to share anything about himself with strangers—even his name.

He turned to the artful display of teas in small wooden chests. 'This is a fine selection,' he said with genuine interest. He was here to glean information for his new project. A hotel completely different from anything he'd created before. He'd been isolated from the hospitality business in the past years and needed to be on top of the trends. He knew all about partying and decadence— what he sought now was restraint and calm. A different way of doing business. A different *life*.

'Tea has become very fashionable,' Adele said in what seemed a purposely neutral voice, more for the benefit of the other woman rather than any conscious desire to engage in conversation with *him*. 'Not any old teas, naturally. Herbal teas, healing tisanes, special blends. I highly recommend the parsnip, ginger and turmeric blend—organic and vegan, which is a good thing.'

Alex gagged at the thought of it.

But if that was what people wanted at a place

like this, it would be up to him to give it to them. Of course Adele would know about what was fashionable in foods and beverages. Her *Dell Dishes* blog attracted an extraordinary number of visitors. Or it had three years ago when he had instructed his lawyers to delve deep into her life with particular reference to her income.

At one stage he had thought about suing her personally as well as via the publishing company that had employed her as a food critic and editor of its restaurant guide. Back then, scrutinising *Dell Dishes*, he hadn't thought she had done enough to monetise her site, to take advantage of the potential appeal to advertisers. Needless to say he hadn't offered her any advice—he'd wanted to bring her down, not help her soar.

'I'll pass on the parsnip tea, thank you,' he said, suppressing a grimace. 'What I want is coffee—strong and black.' He couldn't keep the yearning from his voice.

'No such thing here, I'm afraid,' she said, with a wry expression that he couldn't help but find cute. *Cute*. It was incomprehensible that he should find Adele Hudson *cute*.

He groaned. 'No coffee at all?'

She shook her head. 'Not part of the "clean food" ethos of the spa. You'll have to sneak out to the Bay Bites café. They serve Dolphin Bay's finest coffee. I can personally vouch for it.'

'I might follow up on that.'

His friends the Morgan brothers, Ben and Jesse, had made the once sleepy beachside town of Dolphin Bay into quite a destination with the critically acclaimed Hotel Harbourside, Bay Bites, Bay Books and now the eco-friendly Bay Breeze spa in which Alex had invested in the early stages. It would not be long before he saw a return on his investment.

The new resort was still in its debut phase but had been an immediate success. It had been booked out for Easter a few weeks back. The Morgans had read the market well. In just one day Alex had picked aspects he liked about the operation and ones he didn't think would translate to his new venture. What worked in Australia might not necessarily work in Greece.

'Escaping for coffee is hardly in the spirit of eating clean food.' Adele sounded stern but there was an unexpected gleam of fun in her eyes. Eyes that were green like the olives growing on the island in the Ionian Sea that had once belonged to his ancestors and that he had bought so it once more was owned by a Mikhalis.

He couldn't help his snort of disgust at her comment. 'So does "clean food" mean that all other food is "dirty"? I don't like the idea of that. Especially the traditional Greek foods I grew up on.'

'I think that term is debatable too,' she said. 'I wonder if—?'

Adele's grey-haired companion chose that moment to pick up her cup of herbal tea and make to move away. 'I want to say again how much I love your blog,' she enthused. 'My daughter told me about it. Even my granddaughter is a fan, and she's still at school.'

Adele flushed and looked pleased. As she

should—it was no mean feat to have her site appeal to three generations. 'Thank you. I hope I can keep on bringing you more of what you enjoy.'

'You'll do that, I'm sure,' the other woman said. 'In the meantime, I'll leave you two to chat.' She departed but not without a speculative look from Alex to Adele and back to him again.

Alex groaned inwardly. He recognised that gleam in her narrowed eyes. The same match-making gleam he'd seen often in the women of his extended Greek family. This particular lady had got completely the wrong end of the stick. He had no romantic interest whatsoever in Adele Hudson. In fact he had no interest in any kind of permanent relationship with any woman— in spite of the pressure from his family to settle down. Not now. Not ever. Not after what he'd endured. Not after what he had *done*.

Besides, Adele was married. Or she had been three years ago. He glanced down at her left hand. *No ring.* So maybe she was no longer married. Not that her marital state was of any interest to him.

Adele had obviously not missed that matchmaking gleam either. When she looked back at him, the undisguised horror in her eyes told him exactly what she thought of the idea of anyone pairing her with *him*.

Alex had taken worse insults in his time. So why did that feel like a kick to the gut? He decided not to linger any longer at the tea station. Or to admit even to himself that he would like lovely Adele Hudson to look at him with something other than extreme distaste.

CHAPTER TWO

THE NEXT TIME Alex saw Adele Hudson he'd beaten her to their mutual destination—the dolphin-themed Bay Bites café that overlooked the picturesque harbour of Dolphin Bay. The café was buzzing with the hum of conversation, the aromas of fresh baking—and that indefinable feeling of a successful business. Alex missed being 'hands on' in his own restaurants so much it ached. That world was what had driven him since he'd been a teenager. Even before that. As a child he'd spent some of his happiest hours in his grandfather's restaurant.

Here he could sense the goodwill of the customers, the seamless teamwork of the staff. All was as he liked it to be in his own establishments. And Adele had been right, the café did have excellent coffee. He was sitting at a table near the window, savouring his second espresso, when he looked up to see her heading his way, pedalling one of the bicycles Bay Breeze provided for guests.

She cycled energetically, a woman on a mission to get somewhere quickly. Her face was flushed from exertion as she got off and slid the bike onto a rack outside the café. She took off her bike helmet and shook out her auburn hair with a gesture of unconscious grace. Her hair glinted with copper highlights in the morning sunlight, dazzling him.

This woman was nothing to him but an old adversary. Yet Alex found it difficult to look away from her fresh beauty. Since he'd been living in Greece, getting back to basics with his family there, he felt as if he were seeing life through new eyes. He was certainly seeing something different in Adele Hudson. Or maybe it had always been there and he'd been so intent on revenge he hadn't noticed. There was something vibrant and uncontrived about her, dressed in white shorts and a simple white top, white sneakers and with a small multicoloured backpack. She radiated energy and good health, her face open and welcome to new experience.

Alex didn't alert her to his presence; she'd notice him soon enough. When she did, her first reaction on catching sight of him was out-and-out dismay, quickly covered up by another forced smile. Again he felt that kick in the gut—quite unjustifiably considering how he'd treated her in the past.

She stopped by his table and he got up to greet her, glad she hadn't just walked by with a cursory nod. 'So you took my advice,' she said. Her flushed cheeks made her eyes seem even greener. Her hair was tousled around her face.

'Yes,' he said. 'I become a raging beast without my coffee.'

It was a bad choice of words. The look that flashed across her eyes told him she found the *beast* label only too appropriate. And that not only did she dislike him, but it seemed she also might fear him.

A jolt of remorse hit him. That was not the reaction he ever wanted from a woman. He thought back to the court case. There'd been some kind of confrontation outside on the day the judge had handed down his decision—although surely nothing to make her frightened of him.

'I'm not partial to raging beasts,' she said. *Beasts like you* were the words she left unspoken but he understand as well as if she had shouted them.

Against all his own legal advice he'd gone after her and the major Sydney newspaper that had published her review. He'd been furious at her criticism of Athina, his first important restaurant—the one that had launched him as a serious contender on the competitive Sydney market. He'd had a lot to prove when he'd closed his grandfather's original traditional Greek restaurant and reopened with something cutting-edge fashionable. The risk had paid off—and success after success had followed. And then she'd published a bad review of Athina, detailing how the prices had gone up and the quality gone down, along with the levels of service. It had seemed like a personal assault.

So much had happened to him since then. His fury at her review now seemed disproportionate—a major overreaction to what the court had found to be fair comment. In light of what had happened during the hostage scenario and its aftermath it seemed insignificant. She had nothing to fear from him. Not now.

He looked directly at her. 'I told you this beast has been tamed,' he said gruffly. It was as much an explanation as he felt able to give her. He didn't share with anyone how he'd had to claw his way out of the abyss.

But her brow furrowed. 'Tamed by the coffee?'

She didn't get what he meant. But he had no intention of spelling out the bigger picture for her. How devastated he'd been by Mia's death. The train wreck his life had become. He'd been a broken man, unable to deal with the public spotlight on him—the spotlight he'd once courted. There had only been the pain, the loss, the unrelenting guilt.

His father had intervened, packed him up and sent him back to the Greek village his grandfather had left long ago to emigrate to Australia. At first, Alex had deeply resented his exile. But the distance and the return to his family's roots had given him a painfully gained new perspective and self-knowledge. He'd discovered he hadn't much liked the man he'd become in Sydney.

The presence of Adele Hudson was like an arrow piercing his armour, reminding him of how invincible he'd thought himself to be back then when he'd been flying so high, how agonising his crash into the shadows. He forced his voice to sound steady and impartial. 'The magical powers of caffeine,' he said. 'Can I order you a coffee?'

Adele gave him a look through narrowed eyes that let him know she realised there was something more to his words that she hadn't grasped. But didn't care to pursue. She peered towards the back of the café to the door that led to the kitchen. 'No, thank you. I've popped in to see Lizzie.'

'Lizzie Dumont?'

Jesse's wife was a chef and the driving force behind the exemplary standards of the Morgan eateries. Alex had tried to poach her to work for him on a start-up in Sydney, a traditional French bistro. That was before he'd realised she'd been engaged to Jesse Morgan. That had stopped him. Back then he'd let nothing stop his quest for success—except loyalty to friends and family. That had never been negotiable.

'She's Lizzie Morgan now, well and truly married to Jesse,' Adele said. 'They have a beautiful baby boy, a brother for her daughter Amy.'

'Yes,' he said.

Lizzie had a child from her first marriage. Alex had admired Jesse for taking on a stepchild. Had admired him the more because it wasn't something Alex himself could ever do. His feeling for family and heritage was too deeply ingrained to ever take on another man's child. He would never date a woman who came encumbered.

'Here she is.' Adele waved at a tall woman with curly, pale blonde hair who had pushed her way through the doors from the kitchen.

'Dell! It's so good to see you.' Alex watched as Lizzie swept Adele up in a hug. 'It's been too long. We've got so much to catch up on.'

'We certainly do,' said Adele, giving Lizzie the full benefit of her dazzling smile. Politely, she turned to include him in the conversation. *No smile for him.* 'Lizzie, I think you know Alex Mik—'

'Of course I do,' Lizzie said. She greeted him with a hug and kisses on both cheeks. 'He's a good friend of Jesse's. When we heard he was going to be in Sydney we invited him down to Bay Breeze. Long time, no see, Alex.' Her smile dimmed and her voice softened. 'Are you okay?'

He nodded. 'As okay as I can be,' he said. 'I've appreciated the support from you and Jesse. It means a lot.' He didn't want to talk about his loss any further. Displaying vulnerability clashed with all the ideals of manhood that had been imbued in him by his family. 'I didn't know you two knew each other,' he said. How much did Lizzie know of his history with Adele? No doubt he'd been painted as an ogre of the first order. *A beast.*

Lizzie beamed. 'Dell was one of our first customers. Her glowing reviews of Bay Bites helped put us on the map. The bonus was we became friends. Though we don't see each other as much as we'd like.'

Adele studiously avoided his eyes, obviously uncomfortable at the mention of her good reviews when she'd given Athina such a stinker. The court case had ensured she'd never reviewed his newer ventures, never put them 'on the map'.

'I've always loved this part of the world,' she said. 'And Bay Breeze is the icing on the cake. I love what you guys have done with it, Lizzie. The building, the fit-out, the food. The timing is perfect. Stress and burnout are endemic today. Offering this kind of retreat in such an awesome natural setting is just what a particular lucrative market is looking for.'

Had she read his mind? She could have been

quoting him on the pitch for his new luxury boutique resort.

As she chatted with Lizzie, Alex was surprised at how much Adele knew about the hospitality business. She was both perceptive and canny. She understood how success came from meeting people's needs but also about anticipating them. Giving them what they didn't know they wanted until it was offered to them, all new and shiny. Knowing your customer through and through. Being open to change and nimble enough to adapt to it.

The strength of Bay Breeze she had pinpointed was on track with what he wanted for his new venue. It wasn't often he met someone who was so in tune with how he thought about the business. Although that was perhaps not such a surprise when in the past he'd surrounded himself with too many 'yes' men.

'So what are your plans for life after the newspaper?' Lizzie asked her.

Adele frowned at Lizzie with what was obviously a warning. Alex realised she didn't want him to hear that. Which made him determined not to miss a word.

'What do you mean?' he asked.

Lizzie sounded outraged. 'That darn newspaper fired Dell. Booted her out with a cheque in lieu of notice.'

Adele glared at her friend for spilling the beans.

'Is that true?' he asked Adele. 'You've lost your job?'

She shrugged. But he could see it was an effort for her to sound casual about such a blow. Especially in front of him. 'Budget cuts, they said. It…it was a shock.'

'Because of the court case?' Regret churned in him. How much damage had he caused for something that now seemed unimportant?

She didn't meet his eye. 'No. That was three years ago. Although I was never popular with management afterwards. Being sued wasn't regarded as a highlight of my résumé.'

He frowned. 'What will you do?' He felt a shaft of shame at what he had put her through.

Although he had felt totally in the right at the time.

Alex expected a snarl and a rejoinder to mind his own business. But she couldn't mask the panic in her eyes. 'I don't know yet. They only gave me the boot a week ago. But I've got options.'

'Of course you have,' said loyal Lizzie. 'Publicity and marketing among them. That would be a logical move for you.'

Adele nodded to her friend. 'Yes, I've thought of that,' she said. 'And I can freelance. It will also allow me to give my blog more attention.'

Alex doubted she could make enough to live on from that blog, in spite of the number of readers it attracted. Unless she'd made big strides with attracting advertising since he'd last looked at *Dell Dishes*.

'Your husband?' he asked after some hesitation. He was sure there'd been a husband.

Her mouth twisted. 'Divorced.' Her chin tilted upward. 'In any case, I don't depend on a man to support me.'

He wouldn't have expected any other response from the feisty food critic. 'Do you have children?'

Something he couldn't read darkened her eyes. She shook her head.

'Then come and work for me.' The words escaped his mouth before he'd had time to think about them. But some of his best decisions had been made on impulse.

Dell looked up at Alex Mikhalis, the man she regarded as the devil incarnate. He towered over her, darkly formidable in black jeans and a black T-shirt that made no secret of his strength, his impressive muscles.

'Did you just offer me a job?' She couldn't keep the disbelief from her voice. From behind her, she heard Lizzie gasp.

'I did,' he said gruffly.

'Why would you do that?'

'You need a job. I need help with a new venture. Your understanding of hospitality is impressive. You have skills in PR and publicity.'

Entitled and arrogant, he so obviously expected an instant 'yes'. But it would not be forthcoming from her. She sympathised with his personal loss. That didn't mean she wanted to work with him. Especially not to be under his control as an employee.

She couldn't think of anything worse.

'I appreciate the offer,' she said. 'But I can't possibly accept. I suspect you know why.'

His legal team had undermined her credibility at every opportunity. Even though her newspaper had won the case, she had come out of it bruised and battered with her reputation intact but shredded around the edges. Even three years later she felt it had influenced her employer into 'letting her go'. And that was apart from the stress it had put on her marriage.

He scowled. 'I want to make amends.'

Alex Mikhalis make amends? To her? She frowned. 'Is this some kind of trick?'

'No tricks,' he said. His voice was deep, assured, confident. Yet did nothing to reassure her.

'I find that difficult to believe. You…you

threatened me. Told me you would get even.' He made her so nervous it was difficult to get her words out. She had heard the rumours of how effectively he had brought down his business opponents. But she would not let him sense her fear.

'That was a different time and place. There is no threat.'

'Why should I trust you?' Memories of his intimidation on the courtroom steps flooded back.

Dell became aware that she and the tall, broad-shouldered man were the focus of interest among the customers of the café. She moved closer to him so she could lower her voice. He moved closer as well. *Too close.* She felt as if he were taking up all the air, making her heart race, her breath come short.

'I'm a different man,' he said, his expression intent, dark eyes unreadable as he searched her face.

He *looked* different, that was for sure. Stripped of designer trappings to a raw masculinity that, in spite of her dislike of him, she could not help but appreciate. As for his nature? Leopards didn't change their spots. And there had always been something predatory about him.

She couldn't help the snort of disbelief that escaped her. 'Huh! You? As if I believe—'

A flash of pain contorted his features but was gone so quickly she might have imagined it if it hadn't made such an impression on her that it stopped her words short. For a long moment she stared up at him. It had been three years since she had faced him on the courtroom steps. He had been through trauma like she couldn't imagine. Who knew how that might have affected him? Maybe he was telling the truth.

She felt a gentle tap on her arm and turned, dazed, to see Lizzie. 'Perhaps you should consider this offer,' her friend said quietly. Her eyes gave her a silent message. *You have debts.*

Dell was only too aware of the debts she had run up during her marriage and that had become her responsibility. Lizzie always gave her wise counsel. Her friend would be horrified if she knew the decision she had made just the week before she had lost her job. If it paid off, she might need a job more than ever. And with so many people reviewing restaurants online for free, she felt the newspaper editor had been telling the truth when he'd told her that her role was redundant. Job offers weren't exactly flooding her inbox. She forced herself to take a deep, calming breath.

Then turned back to face Alex. 'Why do you want to make amends?' she said. 'And what makes you think we could work together? I'm a writer, not a restaurateur.'

'I'll answer both your questions with one reply,' he said. 'Every criticism you made about my restaurant Athina was true. My manager was systematically defrauding me. Your judgement was spot on. I should have taken your review as a warning instead of taking you to court.'

'Oh,' was all she was able to choke out. Alex Mikhalis admitting he was *wrong*?

A ghost of a smile lifted the corners of his mouth. She was more used to seeing him glare and scowl at her. The effect was disconcerting.

A devil undoubtedly. But a fiendishly handsome devil. For the first time she saw a hint of the legendary charisma that had propelled him to such heights in a people-pleasing business.

'I've shocked you speechless,' he said.

'I admit it. I'm stunned. After all that…that angst. When did you find out?'

'When I slipped back into Sydney for the review of the police handling of the siege,' he said, now without any trace of a smile.

Dell nodded, unable to find the words to say anything about what must have been such a terrible time in his life. The saga had made headlines in the media for weeks. 'From my memory, the manager was your friend,' she said instead.

'Yes,' he said simply.

How betrayed he must have felt on top of everything else he'd had to endure.

'Perhaps if I had been an investigative reporter I might have discovered that,' she said.

'I wouldn't have believed you. Everything in your review pointed that way. I just didn't see it.'

'Didn't *want* to see it, perhaps,' she said.

He paused, then the words came slowly. 'I…
I'm sorry, Adele.'

Alex Mikhalis *apologising*? After all this man
had put her through?

She thought again about all *he* had been
through since. Realised she was intrigued at the
thought of what project he might be working on
now. And that it wasn't healthy to hold a grudge
or wise to refuse an apparently sincere apology.
Especially when she really needed a job. Lizzie
was right. She should consider this.

'Dell,' she said. 'Please call me Dell. Adele
is my newspaper byline, the name on my birth
certificate.' She looked up at him. 'Tell me more
about this job.'

CHAPTER THREE

ALEX DIDN'T KNOW why it had suddenly become so important that Adele Hudson—Dell—accept his impromptu job offer. But he didn't question it. Much of his success in business had come from following his instinct and he'd learned not to ignore its prompts.

Dell could be just the person he needed to help him launch his new project. The project he needed to get him back on track with life.

Mentally, he checked off the skills she brought to the table. Without a doubt she was good with words—a huge asset for launching into a new market. Another strength was she saw the hospitality industry through the eyes of the customer while at the same understanding how the business side operated. Her blog gave her an international view with access to readers all around the world. On top of that, she was smart and perceptive.

Her review of Athina had raised red flags he should have heeded. His traitorous so-called friend had been doing illicit deals with suppliers and siphoning off funds to a private bank account. He would have saved himself a good deal of money if he hadn't let pride and anger blind him to the truth of what she had observed.

Since he'd been back living in the land of his ancestors he had thought a lot about the Ancient Greek concept of fate. Was it his selfishness or fate that had put Mia in his city restaurant when a sociopath had decided to make a deadly statement? Could it be that fate had brought Dell back into his life? Right at the time when he needed help to launch something different and she was in need of a job? At a time when he was growing weary of punishing himself for something that had been out of his control.

Dell looked up at him, her green eyes direct. 'What exactly does the job entail?' she asked.

Fact was, there wasn't a job vacancy as such. He would create a role for her.

Alex looked around the café, filling up now as lunchtime approached. Lizzie had left them to return to the kitchen. 'We need to go somewhere more private where we can talk.'

Dell nodded with immediate understanding. 'What about the harbour front?' she said.

He put cash on the table to cover both his coffee and a very generous tip. 'Good idea.'

He followed her out of the café. She looked good in shorts with her slender legs and shapely behind. In fact she was downright sexy. How had he not noticed that sensuous sway before? Alex forced his gaze away. *This was about business.*

He walked with her past the adjoining bookstore towards a lookout with a view across the stone-walled harbour with its array of fishing and pleasure craft. The scene was in some ways reminiscent of the fishing village his Greek ancestors came from, in others completely different.

He'd been born and grown up in Australia and thought of himself as Australian. But his Greek heritage was calling to him. He was back here just for a quick visit to help celebrate his father's sixtieth birthday and to take a look at Bay Breeze. Greece was where he wanted to be right now. He didn't think he could ever live back in Sydney again. Not with the memories and regrets that assaulted him at every turn.

'No one will overhear us here,' Dell said when they reached the lookout. 'Fire away.'

He looked around to be sure. His success hadn't come about by sharing his strategies. 'I would usually require you to sign a confidentiality agreement before discussing a new project.'

She shrugged. 'I'm good with that. Just tell me where to sign.'

Through his dealings with her as an adversary he'd also come to a grudging admiration of her honesty. According to the judge, her review had been scrupulously within the boundary of fair comment. And his lawyers had been unable to dig up even a skerrick of dirt on her.

'I wasn't expecting this, so I don't have an agreement with me,' he said.

'You can trust me,' she said. 'I'm good at keeping secrets.'

He had been accused of being a ruthless and cynical businessman—never taking anyone on trust. Yet instinct told him he could talk to this woman without his plans being broadcast where they shouldn't.

Still…he hadn't changed *that* much. 'I'll email a document to you when I'm back at the resort.'

'Of course,' she said with a tinge of impatience. 'I'll sign it straight away. But right now I'm dying of curiosity about the role you have in mind for me.'

Alex leaned back against the railing. 'I'm not at Bay Breeze for the yoga and the parsnip tea,' he said.

Dell's green eyes danced with amusement. 'I kind of got that,' she said.

'I'm a stakeholder and I wanted to see what my investment has got me. The more I'm involved, the more I like the well-being concept. It seems right for the times.' And for *his* time.

'You want to start a similar kind of resort?'

He nodded. 'It's already under way. On a private island. Upscale. Exclusive. To appeal to the top end of the market. But my experience is all in restaurants and nightclubs. A resort is something different and challenging. I need some help.' Alex had to force out the final words. He never found it easy to admit he needed help in anything. Had always seen it as a weakness.

'That's where I come in?'

He nodded. 'But I don't have a job description for the role. I wasn't expecting someone like you to come along at this stage.'

'You mean you're making the job up as you go along?'

She was direct. There was another thing he'd found interesting about Dell during their legal stoush. He added another, less tangible asset to the list of her attributes. *He would enjoy working with her.*

'Yeah. I am. Which is good for you as I can

shape the role to your talents. I have input from top designers and consultants for the building and fit-out. I've got my key hospitality staff on contract. But I want someone to work with me on fine-tuning the offer to guests and with the publicity. Establishing an exclusive well-being resort on a private island is something different for me.'

'That is quite a challenge,' she said.

'Yes,' he said. And a much-needed distraction. He'd go crazy if he didn't throw himself into a big, all-consuming project.

He'd thought he could walk away from his business. The business he blamed for Mia's death. She'd been a chef in one of his restaurants when he'd met her. There had been a strict company rule against fraternising between staff in his businesses. He'd instigated it and he'd broken it when he'd become beguiled by Mia. They'd been living together—her pushing for marriage, he putting it off—when the chef at his busiest city lunchtime venue had been injured in an accident on the way to work. Mia was having a rostered day off. Alex had pulled rank and insisted she go into work that day to replace the chef. He could not take that memory out again, to pick and prod at it, a wound that would never heal.

Since he'd been away, he'd discreetly sold off his Sydney venues one by one. All except Athina. He couldn't bear to let his inheritance from his grandfather go. Financially he never needed to work again. But he *had* to work. He hadn't realised how much his work had defined him until he hadn't had it to occupy himself day after lonely day.

Dell's auburn brows drew together in a frown. 'Why me? There must be more experienced people around who would jump at the chance to work with you on such a project.'

He didn't want to mention fate or kismet or whatever it was that had sent her here. The hunch that made him think she was what he needed right now. 'But it's you I want. And you need a job.'

'The role does interest me,' she said cautiously.

'Although I'd want to keep my blog. It's important to me.'

'I see your blog as an asset, complementary to your work with me,' he said. 'You could utilise it for soft publicity, along with social media.'

She nodded. 'I'll consider that.'

'I'm thinking the title of Publicity Director,' he said. He named a handsome salary.

She blinked. 'That definitely interests me,' she said.

'I pay well and expect utmost commitment in return.'

'I have no issue with that,' she said. 'I've been described more than once as a workaholic.'

Her mouth set in a rigid line and he wondered if it was the ex-husband who had criticised her. He remembered wondering why he hadn't been at court to support his wife during the case. 'Truth is, if I get really involved, the line between work and interest blurs,' she said.

As it always had with him. 'I think you'll find this interesting,' he said. 'The project is under way but the best is yet to come. You'd be coming on board at an exciting time. I want to open in June.'

Her eyes widened. 'It's already April. Isn't that leaving it late?'

'Agree. It's cutting it fine. I won't expect full occupancy until next year.'

'When would you want me to start?' she asked. He could sense her simmering excitement. 'Because I'm firing with ideas already.'

'A week. Two weeks max.'

She smiled. 'I could do that.' That big embracing smile was finally aimed at him. For a moment, he had to close his eyes against its dazzle. 'I love the idea of an exclusive private island. Where is it? North of Sydney? Queensland? South Australia?'

He shook his head. 'Greece.'

'*Greece?* I…I wasn't expecting that.'

Alex had expected her to react with excitement. Not a clouding of her eyes and a disappointed turn down of her mouth. He frowned.

'My island of Kosmima is in northern Greece where my ancestors come from. Where I've been living with my Greek family since I left Australia. The most beautiful private island in the Ionian Sea. I'm sure you would love it.'

Of course she would love it.

Dell had always wanted to visit Greece. It had held a fascination for her since she'd studied ancient history at school. The mythology. The history. The ancient buildings. She wanted to climb the Acropolis in Athens to see the Parthenon. To visit the picturesque islands with their whitewashed buildings and blue roofs. There was nowhere in the world she wanted to visit more than Greece.

But travel had long been off the cards. She'd committed young to her high-school boyfriend and been caught up in mortgages and marriage to a man who hadn't had an ounce of wanderlust in him. She'd travelled some with her parents and longed to travel more. Even to live abroad one day.

But there was something else she'd wanted

more. Wanted so desperately she'd put all her other dreams on hold to pursue it.

'I…assumed the job was in Australia,' she said.

He shook his head. 'No new venues in Australia for the foreseeable future. Europe is where I want to be. But I'd like a fellow Australian on board with me. Someone who knows about my businesses here, understands how things operate. In other words, you.'

So this was how it felt when big dreams collided.

Dell swallowed hard against the pain of her disappointment. 'I'm very sorry, but I'm going to have to say no to your job offer. I can't possibly go to Greece.'

His dark eyebrows rose in disbelief. She had knocked back what anyone might term a dream job. *Her* dream job. She suspected Alex wasn't used to people saying no to him. But there was disappointment too in those black eyes. He had created a role just for her, tailored to her skills.

She was grateful for the confidence he had put in her ability.

But she couldn't tell him why she had to turn down the most enticing offer she was ever likely to get. Why she couldn't be far away from home. That there was a chance she might be pregnant.

CHAPTER FOUR

WHEN DELL HAD been a little girl and people asked her what she wanted to be when she grew up, she had always replied she wanted to be a mummy. They had laughed and asked what else, but she had stubbornly stood her ground.

She didn't know why, as heaven knew her mother hadn't been particularly maternal. And her father had verged on the indifferent. Both her parents had been—still were—research scientists for multinational pharmaceutical companies. She suspected they would have been happy to stop at the one child, her older brother, and when she'd come along when he'd been five she'd been more of an inconvenience than a joy. Her brother was of a scientific bent like her parents. She, while as intelligent, had broader interests they didn't share or understand.

As a child, Dell had loved her dolls, her kitten, her books and food. Her mother was a haphazard cook and by the time she was twelve Dell had been cooking for the family. It became a passion.

At the insistence of her parents, she had completed a degree in food science. A future in the laboratory of a major grocery manufacturer beckoned. Instead, to the horror of her parents, after graduation she went straight to work as an editorial assistant on a suburban newspaper. She showed a flair for restaurant reviewing and articles about food and lifestyle and her career went on from there.

At twenty-two, she married Neil, her high-school boyfriend. He supported her in her desire to become a mother. That was when her plans derailed. In spite of their most energetic efforts, pregnancy didn't happen. At age twenty-seven they started IVF. The procedure was painful and disruptive. The hormone treatments sent her emotions soaring and plunging. The joy went out of her love-life. But three expensive IVF procedures didn't result in pregnancy. Just debt.

Then Neil had walked out on her.

Growing up, Dell had often felt like a fluffy, colourful changeling of a chick popped into the nest of sleek, clever hawks who had never got over their surprise in finding her there. She had become adept at putting on a happy face when she'd felt misunderstood and unhappy.

The end of her marriage had come from left field and she'd been devastated. She'd loved Neil and had thought she'd be married for ever. She shared her tears with a few close friends but presented that smiling, fluffy-chick face to the world.

Being suddenly single came as a shock. She'd been part of a couple for so long she didn't know how to deal with dating. After a series of disastrous encounters she'd given up on the idea of meeting another man. Work became her solace as she tried to deal with the death of her big dream. Accepted that, if IVF hadn't worked, she wasn't likely to ever be a mother.

Then just weeks ago the fertility clinic had

called to ask what she wanted them to do with the remaining embryo she had stored with them.

Dell knew she should have told them she was divorced. That her ex-husband was in another relationship. But they didn't ask and she didn't tell. She'd undergone the fourth procedure the week before she'd been fired. All her other attempts at IVF had failed. She hadn't held out any real hope for this time. But she'd felt compelled to grab at that one final chance.

Now, the day after her meeting with Alex Mikhalis, Dell lay back on her cool white bed at Bay Breeze racked by the cramps that had always heralded failure. She took in a great, gasping sob then stayed absolutely still, desperately willing that implant to stay put. Her baby. But a visit to the bathroom confirmed blood. She'd failed again.

She would never be a mother.

Dell stood at the window for a long time staring sightlessly out to the view of the sea. Her hand rested on her flat, flat stomach. There was nothing for her here. No job. No man. No close family. Just parents who, if she left the country, would wave her goodbye without thinking to ask why she was going. Her friends were starting families and moving into a life cycle she couldn't share. She hadn't told anyone about this last desperate effort to conceive so there was no one to share her grief. But she did have all her cyber friends on her blog. She had to put on her fluffy-chick face and move on.

Without thinking any further, she picked up the house phone and called through to Alex Mikhalis's room. She braced herself to leave a message and was shocked when he answered. Somehow she found the words to ask could she have a meeting with him. His tone was abrupt as he told her to be quick—he was packing to head back to Sydney.

Dell had no chance to change. Or apply makeup. Just pushed her hair into place in front of the mirror and slicked on some lip gloss. Yoga pants were *de rigueur* in a place like this anyway. He wouldn't expect to see her in a business suit and heels.

He answered the door to his room. 'Yes?' he said, his voice deep and gruff and more than a touch forbidding.

For a long moment Dell hesitated on the threshold. He towered over her, in black trousers and a charcoal-grey shirt looking every inch the formidable tycoon. Half of the buttons on his shirt were left open, as if he'd been fastening them when she'd sounded the buzzer on his door. It left bare a triangle of olive skin and a hint of dark chest hair on an impressively muscled chest.

Her heart started to beat double-quick time and she felt so shaky at the knees she had to clutch at the doorframe for support. Not because she was nervous about approaching him. Or feared what kind of a boss he might be. No. It was because her long-dormant libido had flared suddenly back into life at the sight of him—those dark eyes, the proud nose, the strong jaw newly shaven but already shadowing with growth. *He was hot.*

Dell swallowed against a suddenly dry mouth.

This unwelcome surge of sensual awareness could complicate things. She was beginning to rethink his devil incarnate status. But who knew if he was sincere about having changed? After all, she'd seen him at his intimidating worst on those courtroom steps. She had to take him on trust but be cautious. That did not mean fancying the pants off him.

Eyes off the gorgeous man, Dell.

He stepped back and she could see his bag half packed on his bed. Perhaps he was headed to Greece and she would never see him again. This could be her only chance.

She forced her lips into a smile, the wobble at the edge betraying her attempt to be both nonchalant and professional. And not let him guess the turmoil of her senses evoked by his half-dressed state. 'Your job offer?' she said.

He nodded.

'Can…can a person change her mind?'

Alex stared at Dell. What had happened? Thinly disguised anguish showed in the set of her jaw, the pallor of her face, her red-rimmed eyes. The expression in her eyes was sad rather than sparkling. But as she met his gaze, her cheeks flushed pink high on her cheekbones, her chin rose resolutely and he wondered if he'd imagined it.

'I'd like to accept the job.' She hesitated. There was an edge to her voice that made him believe he had not imagined her distress. 'That is, if the position is still on offer.'

Alex had been gutted when she'd turned him down. Disappointed out of all proportion. And stunned that he'd been so shaken. Because of course she'd been right. Whisper a word in a recruitment agent's ear and he'd be inundated with qualified people ready to take up the job with him. Why Dell Hudson? Because it was her and only her he'd wanted. He'd had no intention of taking her 'no' as final. In fact he'd been planning strategies aimed at getting a 'yes' from her.

Once he'd made up his mind about something it was difficult to budge him. It was a trait he had inherited from his stubborn grandfather. No one else would do but *her*. Was it his tried and tested gut feel telling him that? Or something else? It was nothing to do with the fact he found her attractive. That was totally beside the point. He did not date employees. Never, ever after what had happened with Mia.

'Why did you change your mind?' he asked Dell.

She took a deep breath, which emphasised the curve of her breasts outlined by her tight-fitting tank top. How had he never noticed how sexy she was? He forced his eyes upward to catch the nuances of her expression rather than the curves of her shapely body.

'A...sudden change of circumstances,' she said. 'Something...something personal.'

'Problems with a guy?' he asked. Over the years he'd learned to deal with the personal dramas of female staff. Not that it ever got easier.

She shook her head and again he caught that glimpse of sadness in her eyes. 'No. I'm one hundred per cent single. And intending to stay that way. I'm free to devote my time entirely to my work with you.'

'Good,' he said. He didn't want to hear the details of her marriage breakup. Or any bust-ups that came afterwards. That was none of his concern. This was about a job. Nothing more.

Although he found it very difficult to believe she was single by choice.

'I don't let my personal life impinge on my work,' she said. 'I want your job and I want to go to Greece.'

'You're sure about that? You're not going to change your mind again?'

She took another distracting deep breath. 'I'm very sure.'

He allowed himself a smile, knowing that it was tinged with triumph. Reached out to shake her hand. 'When can you be ready to fly to Athens?'

CHAPTER FIVE

SHE WAS IN GREECE, working for Alex Mikhalis!

It had all happened so fast Dell still felt a little dizzy that, just two weeks after her wobbly encounter with him in the yoga room, the man who had been her adversary—the man she had loathed—was her boss.

So far so good. It had been a long, tedious trip to get here even in the comfort of the business-class seats he had booked for her—twenty-three hours to Athens alone. Then another short flight to the small airport at Preveza in north-western Greece.

Too excited to be jet-lagged, she staggered out into the sunshine expecting to find a sign with her name on it held up by a taxi driver. But her new boss was there to meet her. Tall and imposing, he stood out among the people waiting for passengers. He waved to get her attention.

Dell's breath caught and her heart started hammering. It was the first time she'd seen Alex since that meeting in his room at Bay Breeze. For a moment she was too stunned to say anything. Not just because her reawakened senses jumped to alert at how Greek-god-handsome he looked in stone linen trousers and a collarless white linen shirt. But because she wasn't sure what rules applied to their changed status. It was quite a leap for her to take from enemy to employee.

'Good flight?' he asked.

'Very good, thank you,' she said, uncertain of what to call him. He was her employer now but they had history of a kind. 'Er…thank you, Mr Mikhalis.'

His dark eyes widened as if she'd said something ridiculous, then he laughed. 'That's my father's name,' he said. 'Alex will do. You're not working for a corporation here. Just me.'

He held out his hand to take hers in a firm,

warm grip. 'Welcome on board.' His handshake was professional, his tone friendly but impersonal. She would take her cue from that. And totally repress that little shiver of awareness that rippled through her at his touch.

'Thank you,' she said. *That was her third 'thank you'.* Their status might have changed but she wondered if she would ever be able to relax around him.

He went to take her luggage and made a mock groan. 'What on earth have you got in here?'

Her suitcase was stuffed to the limit—she'd had no real idea of what she'd be facing and had packed for any occasion. 'Just clothes and…er… shoes.'

'Enough to shoe a centipede by the weight of it,' he said. But he smiled and she felt some of the tension leave her shoulders.

'There's snorkelling equipment there too,' she said a tad defensively. She knew this wouldn't be a regular nine-to-five job but she hoped there'd be leisure time too.

'The waters around the island are perfect for

snorkelling,' he said. 'But the water temperature is still too cold to swim without a wetsuit. It warms up towards the end of May. I'll swim every day then.'

A vision came from nowhere of him spearing through aqua waters, his hair slicked dark to his head, his body lean and strong and muscular, his skin gilded by shafts of sunlight falling through the water. *This was all kinds of crazy.* She forced the too personal thoughts away and thought sensible work-type thoughts. The *only* kind of thoughts she could allow herself to have about him.

What kind of boss would he be?

He'd had a reputation for being somewhat of a tyrant in Sydney. There were rumours of banks of CCTVs in his most popular venues to ensure he could monitor the staff at all times. Spying on them, according to disgruntled employees. Alex's explanation had been the surveillance was there to ensure drinks weren't being spiked with date rape drugs. She hadn't known who to believe at the time.

She followed him to his car. In Sydney at the time of the trial, he had driven the latest model Italian sports car, as befitted his wealthy, playboy image. Now she was surprised to see a somewhat battered four-by-four. Effortlessly he swung her heavy luggage in the back.

'Next stop is Lefkada,' he said. 'You'll be staying at a villa in the port of Nidri and coming over daily by boat to Kosmima.'

Dell already knew that Kosmima was the small private island he owned and the site of his new resort. 'I can't wait to see it,' she said, avid for more information.

As soon as she was settled in the front seat, she launched into a string of questions. She listened as he explained the size of the island—about one thousand metres by one and a half thousand metres. That it was largely untamed vegetation of cypress and oak and a cultivated olive grove. Past owners had turned old donkey trails into accessible roads. The most recent had put in a helipad.

But his deep sonorous voce had a hypnotic

effect. Dell was interested—intensely interested—but she had been awake for more than
thirty hours. She only kept her eyes open long
enough to leave the airport behind and to cross
the causeway that connected Lefkada to the
mainland.

She woke up, drowsy, to find the car station-
ary. For a moment she didn't know where she
was. An unfamiliar car. An unfamiliar view
through the window. *An unfamiliar man.*

Dell froze, suddenly wide awake. In her sleep
she had leaned across from her seat and was
snuggled up to Alex Mikhalis's shoulder. Mor-
tified, she snapped her eyes shut again before he
realised she was awake. *What to do?* She was
aware of a strong, warm body, a spicy masculine scent, his breath stirring her hair—and that
she liked it very much. She liked it too much.
He was her boss.

She pretended to wake with a gasp and scooted
across the seat away from him as fast as her
bottom would take her. 'I'm so sorry,' she said,
aware of the sudden flush staining her cheeks.

That short, nervous laugh she was forever trying to control forced its way out. 'How unprofessional of me.'

His eyes met hers, dark, inscrutable, as he searched her face. She swore her heart stopped with the impact of his nearness. *He was gorgeous.* But she could not let herself acknowledge that. This inconvenient attraction had to be stomped on from the start. She needed this job and could not let anything jeopardise it.

He shrugged broad shoulders. 'Jet lag. It happens to the best of us.' But not everyone used their boss's shoulder as a pillow. 'Don't worry about it,' he said as if he'd scarcely noticed her presence. As if it happened all the time.

No doubt he'd been used to women flinging themselves at him. That was, of course, before he'd lost his fiancée, the lovely chef who had worked for him. The story of their tragic romance had been repeated by the press over and over after she'd died. Everywhere he'd looked he must have seen her face. Such an intensity of loss. No wonder he'd escaped the country.

She realised she was doing the same thing. Running from loss of a different kind but painful just the same. Every month she'd been just a day late she'd hoped she was pregnant. Before each IVF procedure she had allowed herself to dream about the baby she would hold in her arms, imagined how he or she would look, thought about names. Then grieved those lost babies who had seemed so real to her. Two pairs of tiny knitted booties, one pink and one blue, had been hidden in a drawer to be taken out and held against her cheek while she dreamed. But not this last failed attempt at IVF. Packing up her possessions to move out of her small rented apartment, she had found the booties and packed them with the clothes she gave away to charity.

'Thank you,' she said. Again. Were *thank you* and *sorry* going to be the key words of this working relationship? *Toughen up, Dell.*

They were parked near a busy harbour. The marina was packed with a flotilla of tall-masted yachts, motor cruisers and smaller craft of all kinds. The waterfront was lined with colourful cafés and restaurants, each fronted by signs proclaiming their specialities. 'This is the port of Nidri,' Alex said.

Dell noticed charter boats and ferries and signs in English and Greek—of which she couldn't understand a word—to the islands of Corfu and Ithaca and Cephalonia. Excitement started to bubble. She really was in Greece. That dream, at least, had come true.

'This is the town where I'm staying?' she said.

'In a villa complex owned by my aunt and uncle. You'll be comfortable there. There are shops, restaurants, lots of night life. My cousin will take you to and from Kosmima by boat.'

'Do you live there too?' she asked. He didn't wear any rings. She hadn't given thought to whether or not he was still single. He could be married for all she knew, he'd done so well to keep out of the gossip columns where he used to be a regular item. A man like him wouldn't be alone—unless by choice.

'I live on Kosmima, by myself,' he said. His tone told her not to ask any more questions.

She might not be an investigative journalist—
she came under the category of lifestyle writer—
but Dell was consumed with curiosity about how
the nightclub prince of Sydney came to be living
in this place. How he had kept his whereabouts
so secret when he had disappeared from Sydney.

'I'll take you to the villa,' he said. 'We'll have
lunch there then you can settle in and get some
sleep before you start work tomorrow.'

Dell wanted to protest that she was ready to
start work right now but of course that would
be ridiculous. Her impromptu nap in his car had
proved that. She needed to get out of the jeans
she'd worn on the plane, shower and then sleep
before she could be of any use to Alex.

She'd been expecting bare cliffs and blind-
ing white buildings accented in bright blue. But
Alex explained that landscape was typical of the
southern Greek islands. This part of Greece had
green, vegetated islands with homes that blended
more into the landscape. The Greek blue was
there all right but in a more subtle way.

The one-bedroom apartment she was to make

her home was in a small complex of attractive white-painted villas with terracotta roofs set around a swimming pool. Tubs of lavender and sweet-scented herbs were placed at every turn. Sad memories would have a hard time following her here.

Her compact apartment was white and breezy with a tiled floor. Dell looked around her in delight. She would be more than comfortable. Even better, her accommodation was part of her salary package. With the generous remuneration Alex had offered her, she hoped she might be able to make a dent in the debt left to her from the IVF. As she showered and then changed into a simple linen dress, she found herself humming and wishing she knew some Greek songs.

New start?

Bring it on.

As soon as Alex's Aunt Penelope and Uncle Stavros had heard he was picking up his new staff member from Australia from the airport, they had insisted he bring her to share a meal with them. The elderly couple lived on site and managed the villas they let out over the summer, one of which he had secured as Dell's accommodation.

They were actually his great aunt and uncle, Penelope being the youngest sister of his grandfather, but no one in the family bothered with that kind of distinction. He hadn't tried to keep track of all the familial layers. It was just enough that his Greek family had welcomed him without judgement when he had arrived, the high flyer from Australia who'd crashed in spectacular manner. Like Icarus of Greek myth he'd melted his wings by flying too high—in Icarus's case to the sun, in his case too much hard living and stress followed by the tragedy with Mia had led to burnout. He'd come here to heal but wasn't sure how he'd ever get his wings back. He hoped the new venture might lead to the growth of new feathers. Because he couldn't stay grounded for ever.

Dell had instantly charmed his aunt and uncle with her winning smile and chatty manner. She seemed to have a gift for making people feel at ease in a natural, unselfconscious way. Even in repose her face looked as if she was on the verge of smiling. Who could help but want to smile back in response? Yet he'd seen her snarl too and knew she could be tough when required. He felt some of the tension relax from his shoulders. It had been the right decision to bring her here. Dell Hudson on his side could be a very good thing.

The table was set up under a pergola that supported a grape vine, its bright new leaves casting welcome shade. Dell's hair flashed bright in the filtered light, her simple blue and white striped dress perfectly appropriate.

It was a typically Greek scene and he marvelled, as he had many times since he'd got here, how quickly he'd felt at home. During school vacations there had been visits with his parents and two sisters. But once he'd taken over Athina, he hadn't had time to make the obligatory trek to Greece, despite the admonishments of his parents.

'Family is everything,' his grandfather had used to say. But it was only now that Alex really appreciated what he had meant. It wasn't that he didn't value his heritage. Or that he didn't love his family back home. But as he was the much-longed-for son after two daughters, too much pressure and expectation had been put on him. His subsequent rebellion had caused ructions that were only now healing. He felt he'd at last made his peace with his father on his recent visit to Sydney.

Now he tucked into his aunt's splendid cooking—sardines wrapped in vine leaves and herbs; lemon and garlic potatoes; and a sublime eggplant salad. The food was reminiscent of his grandfather's old Athina, not surprising when the recipes had probably been handed down from the same source. Dell chatted and laughed with his aunt and uncle over lunch, as if they were already friends.

'I'm asking your Thia Penelope if I can interview her about her cooking for my blog,' Dell said.

'I am teaching her Greek,' his aunt interjected.

'I'm keen to learn.' Dell smiled at the older lady. 'I've never tasted eggplant cooked as deliciously as this. It's a revelation. That is, if I'm allowed to tell my readers that I'm living in Greece.'

'Why not?' he said, bemused by the fact his aunt had taken it upon herself to teach his newest employee the language. 'Just don't mention the new venture yet.'

'Sure, this will be a subtle way of leading into it,' she said. 'When the time is right it will be fun to reveal exactly what I'm doing here. Right now I'll say I'm on vacation.'

His aunt beamed, her black eyes almost disappearing into the wrinkles around her eyes. 'She's a clever girl, this one,' she said. As she said it she looked from him to Dell and back again.

There it was again—that matchmaking gleam. Just because he was single and his aunt had ascertained that Dell was single. Even though his aunt knew the story of how Mia had died. How responsible he felt for her death. How he did not want—did not deserve—to have love in his life again.

Dell blushed and looked down at her plate. The speculation must be annoying for her too.

'That she is, Auntie,' he said. 'Which is why I've employed her to work with me on the hotel.' He had to make it clear to his family that his relationship with Dell was strictly a working one. He had to keep reminding himself too.

On the drive from the airport she had got drowsier and drowsier as she'd tried to keep up the conversation through her jet lag. Her responses had dwindled to the odd word in answer to something he'd said minutes before and quite out of context. If he knew her better, he'd tease her about it.

But he would not tease her about the way, when she'd fallen fully asleep, she'd slid across her seat to rest her head on his shoulder. Because instead of pushing her away, as she'd murmured something unintelligible in her sleep he'd smiled and without thinking dropped a light kiss on her head. He'd been without a woman for too long. It was the only explanation for his lapse.

That could not happen again.

CHAPTER SIX

THE NEXT MORNING Dell stood on the expansive front balcony of Alex's new resort building on the private island of Kosmima and looked around her in awe. There wasn't another building in sight—just the jetty that belonged to the island.

Below her, the waters of the Ionian Sea sparkled in myriad tones of turquoise as they lapped on the white sands of the bay. She breathed in air tinged with salt and the scent of wild herbs. The bay was bounded by pale limestone cliffs and hills covered in lush vegetation. The sky was a perfect blue with only the odd cloud scudding across the horizon. She felt almost overcome by the natural beauty of the site as she felt the tension and angst of the last weeks start to melt away.

Her new boss stood beside her—waiting, she suspected, with a degree of impatience for her verdict. She turned to him. 'It's every bit as perfect as you said. Magical.'

Alex nodded slowly. 'I think so too. It makes me believe that people have been feeling the magic for hundreds of years. Thousands, perhaps.'

They stood in silence for a long moment, looking out to sea. Was he, like her, imagining the pageant of history that must have been played out on and near these islands?

'Do you know anything about the history of this island?' she asked. 'Any chance it was the site of an ancient Greek temple? That would be useful for publicity.'

'It could also mean Kosmima could be declared as a site of archaeological significance and business prohibited. So I don't think we'll go there,' he said.

'I hadn't thought of that,' she said. 'Maybe we should stick to the de-stressing and well-being angle. Just taking in this view is making me feel relaxed. Although not too relaxed to start work, of course. Tell me what you need me to do. I'm raring to start.'

'First thing is to inspect the site.'

Dell turned and looked back at the magnificent white building that sat stepped back into the side of the hill. It was modern in its simplicity but paid homage to traditional architecture. 'I expected something only half constructed but you must be nearly ready to open.'

'On first sight you might think so, but there's still a way to go before we welcome the first guests in June. This main building was initially built as a private residence. It was very large, but needed alteration and additions to make it fit for the purpose.'

The building was light and airy, luxurious in pale stone with bleached timber woodwork and marble floors. Expansive windows took full advantage of the view, to be shuttered in the colder months. From the back of the building she could hear the construction crew who had been here since early morning.

The last thing she wanted to do was remind Alex of the car journey from the airport. But she couldn't pretend to know important details she had missed while snoozing. 'In the car yesterday you were telling me about the background of this place. But I…I'm afraid I didn't hear it all.'

'Really?' he said, dark brows raised. 'You don't recall anything?'

'Er…I remember the geographical details.'

'Before you fell asleep, you mean?'

'Yes,' she admitted, unable to meet his eyes.

'Was I so boring?' he said.

'No! Not boring at all.' In fact, she'd never met a man less boring. Who would have thought she might be actually growing to like the man who had been so vile during the court case? A man she'd considered an entitled, arrogant playboy who in the short time she'd known him seemed anything but that.

Now she did look up to find his black eyes gleaming with amusement. 'I soon realised you were drowsing off.'

And falling all over him.

How utterly mortifying. But she would not say the sorry word again. 'I do recall something about a billionaire,' she said. 'I promise I'm over the jet lag and wide awake and listening.'

She followed him into the high-ceilinged living space destined to be the 'silent' room where guests could meditate or just be quiet with their thoughts without interruption. Their voices echoed in the unlived silence.

'There was an older, traditional house on this site when the island was owned by a very wealthy Greek industrialist,' he said. 'He and his family used it as a summer retreat. Some members of my family were tenant farmers on the island. Others were employed as gardeners and caretakers.'

'So there's a personal connection?' She was still looking for angles for publicity.

'Yes,' he said. 'The owner was a benevolent landlord who, for all the opulence, never forgot his peasant roots. There were many good years for my family.' He paused. 'I've only found out all this since I've been living in Greece.'

'I guess it wasn't relevant when you were building your empire in Sydney.'

'Correct,' he said. 'I hardly knew this side of my family. Just my grandfather, my father's father, emigrated. The rest of the family stayed here. I only visited a few times back with my parents, the last when I was a teenager.'

'So how did you come to buy the island?'

'The Greek owner died and it was left to a nephew in Athens who had no use for it. He sold it to a Russian billionaire who demolished the house to build this summer palace.'

The tone of his voice told her that the transfer of ownership might not have been good news. 'What happened to your family?'

'They were evicted. The new owner wanted utter privacy. The only staff to live on the island were the ones he brought with him. The island is only accessed by sea. He installed a heliport, and armed guards patrolled the coastline. The construction crews were escorted on and off the island. Every delivery was scrutinised.'

'That's scary stuff. Was there any real threat?'

She wasn't quite sure how she could work that into a press release.

He shrugged. 'Who knows? The locals were pragmatic. They got used to it. The development brought employment—much needed in Greece as you probably know. The good thing is the guy was passionate about sustainability and brought those organic principals to the new build. That was good for me when I took over.'

'So how did you end up owning the island?'

'The owner decamped with the mega-residence unfinished. No one ever found out why, although as you can imagine there were all sorts of rumours. Then the island went up for sale again.'

'What made you buy it?'

'Impulse.'

'You bought an entire island on *impulse*?'

Of course, he'd been a multimillionaire while he was still in his twenties. Why wouldn't he? And if his past history had anything to do with it, the impulse would pay off in return on investment.

'I've always operated on instinct. It seemed the right thing to do.'

There was an edge to his voice but Dell wasn't sure how deep she should dig into his motives. Escape. Retreat. Heal. Even giving back to the land of his ancestors at a time when investment was desperately needed.

But once they started to generate publicity for his new venue, it would be inevitable his personal tragedy would come to the fore. She would carefully suggest they work with it rather than hope it would stay buried. Perhaps a few carefully negotiated exclusives might be the way to go.

The story of the crazed gunman holding Alex's lovely fiancée and a number of customers hostage in a robbery gone wrong had travelled around the world. That the handsome hotelier had sought refuge from his grief in the islands of his ancestors and built a resort there would generate good publicity. But she didn't feel ready to raise it with him just yet. She would have to learn to read him first.

As Alex continued his tour Dell continued to be impressed by everything she saw—kitchen, spa treatment areas, guestrooms, an office area with Wi-Fi and computers. When he asked her opinion she gave it honestly. Better to have areas of potential weakness sorted now rather than after the retreat opened. His venues in Sydney had won design awards. This one would no doubt be clocking up some wins too.

'You certainly know your stuff,' she said. 'I realise you've got a ton of experience in Sydney, but it must be very different doing remodelling and a fit-out in a different country. Where did you find the architects and interior designers?'

'That's where having an extended Greek family helps. My cousins in Athens were able to point me to the right people.'

'And furnishings?' Many of the rooms were still bare.

'In the hands of the designers. Most of it is being made to measure and exclusive to this resort. I need to go to Athens next week. I'd like you to come with me.'

'I would be pleased to,' she said. A ripple of excitement ran through her. 'Just one thing. Would it be possible to time it before I have a day off? I'd love to stay in Athens overnight so I could climb the Acropolis and see the Parthenon. It's something I've always wanted to do. Then I'd like to spend some time in the Acropolis Museum. I've heard it's wonderful.'

'It is spectacular,' he said. 'I'm not what you'd call a museum kind of guy. But when you're seeing all the antiquities and then look up to see the Parthenon through the windows it's quite something.'

Alex spoke with pride of the museum. He looked Greek, spoke like an Australian. Yesterday he'd been too well-mannered to speak more than a few words of Greek to his aunt and uncle in front of her. But he had sounded fluent. She wondered what country he now identified with. Again she felt it was too personal for her to ask him. His grief must run very deep to have left everything familiar behind.

The tour ended outside with a beautiful aquamarine swimming pool, landscaped around with palm trees and bougainvillea. 'Was the pool already here?' she asked.

'Yes. It's big for a private residence but not outstanding for a hotel. I considered extending it but—'

'Why bother when you have the sea on the doorstep?' she said.

'Exactly.' He met her eyes and they both smiled at the same time. It wasn't the first time today that they'd finished each other's words. She felt she was in tune with his vision and it gave her confidence that she would be able to do a good job for him. She held his gaze for a moment too long before she hastily switched her focus.

Set well back from the pool and completely private was an elegant pavilion, the design of which, with its columns and pediments, gave more than a nod to classical Greek architecture. 'Was the pool house here, too?'

He nodded. 'It's a self-contained apartment and where I'm living.'

'It looks fabulous.'

Dell wondered if he would show her around his personal residence. She ached with curiosity to see inside where he spent his private time.

But he took her around to the southern side of the building where there were substantial kitchen gardens and a greenhouse full of early tomatoes. Mature fig, pomegranate, fruit and nut trees were planted behind—spring blossom surrendering to new leaves so green they seemed fluorescent. From their size, she assumed the trees had been there since the days of the Greek owner. Maybe longer.

'How wonderful,' she breathed.

'I've employed the gardeners who used to work here. We intend to grow as much fresh produce as possible,' he said.

'I couldn't think of anything better,' she said. 'It's early days for me planning the food, but I really think the core of the food offering should be based on the Mediterranean diet. I mean mainly plant-based from this garden, olive oil from your grove, fish from these waters, white cheese and yogurt—could you keep goats here, chickens?—

with lots of fruit. Food like your aunt's baked eggplant based on traditional recipes handed down in your family. Maybe some of the daring new twists to old favourites that you served at Athina. Greek dishes interpreted in an Australian way, which would be a point of difference. Of course you'll also have to cater for allergies and intolerances as well as whatever faddy ways of eating are in fashion. The juice bar is essential, and the fancy teas.' She indicated the vegetable garden with an enthusiastic wave. 'But the heart of it starts here. The locavore movement at its best. It checks the boxes for locally grown and "clean", whatever you like to call it. This resort will be an organic part of this island, not *on* it but *of* it.'

Dell faltered to a halt as she realised she'd held the floor for too long, having scarcely paused for breath. 'Er…that is if you think so too…'

He stood watching her, dark eyes enigmatic, before he broke into a slow smile. 'That's exactly what I think,' he said.

Dell felt as breathless as if she'd run a long

race. It seemed she'd passed a test of some sort. After all, he'd acquired her on an impulse too. She kept up to date with food trends. She had a degree in food science, which had covered commercial food preparation. She had critiqued a spectrum of restaurants and resorts in Sydney. But that wouldn't have mattered a flying fig if she hadn't proved herself to be on the same wavelength as Alex when it came to his project.

'That's a relief,' she said. 'I do tend to go on when I'm…passionate about something.'

He smiled again, teeth white against his olive skin, eyes warm. His shirt was open at the neck, rolled up to show tanned forearms. Had a man ever looked better in a white shirt? It would be only too easy to get passionate about *him*.

'Don't ever hold back,' he said. 'I like your enthusiasm. It energises me.'

Passion, energy, his eyes focused on her, his hands—

She couldn't go there.

She took a deep, steadying breath. 'One more

thing,' she asked. 'Have you decided on a name for the resort?'

'Pevezzo Athina,' he said without hesitation. '*Pevezzo* in the local dialect means "safe haven". That's what I want it to be: a haven from life's stresses for our guests.'

And for you too, Dell thought.

'Why the name Athina again?' she said. 'In homage to your restaurant in Sydney?' She felt uncomfortable mentioning it, considering their history.

'That restaurant was named by my grandfather after the *taverna* on the adjoining island, Prasinos, which was run by his parents. It's still there. Pappouli left his home for a better life in Australia. The seas here were becoming overfished and he found it difficult to make a living as a fisherman. He wanted more. I'm named after that grandfather, in the Greek way.'

Dell took up the story. 'So he started Athina restaurant in the city, serving traditional Greek food. It was a great success. First with other migrants like himself and then the Australian business people caught on to how good the food was and it became an institution.'

'You know a lot about it. Of course you do. Because of the—'

'The court case,' she said. No point in avoiding the elephant lurking in the garden.

'What you did not realise—what no one outside our family knew—was how important Athina was to me personally.'

'You defended it so…so fiercely.'

'You mean irrationally?'

'I didn't say that,' she said, her voice dwindling away. But she meant it and he knew it.

'My grandfather came to Australia with nothing, unable to speak more than a few words of English. He ended up successful and prosperous. His kids became professionals—my father is an orthopaedic surgeon, his sister a dermatologist. All thanks to Athina. As a kid, I spent happy times with my *pappouli* and my *yia-yia* at the restaurant. I'd get underfoot in the kitchens, annoy the chefs with questions. Helped out as a waiter as soon as I was old enough.'

'So that's where your interest in restaurants started.' An image of what a dear little boy he must have been flashed into her mind. But she pushed it away. Neil had been dark-haired and dark-eyed—the image of Alex as a child came way too close to what her longed-for babies might have looked like. She had to put that dream behind her.

'I didn't want to be a chef. I wanted to be the boss.' He smiled, an ironic twist of his mouth. 'That's what comes of being the only son in a Greek family. But the pressure was on for me to be a doctor, to keep the migrant dream alive of being upwardly socially mobile. I enrolled in medicine. Loved the social life at uni, the classes were not where I wanted to be. My parents were not happy, to say the least.'

'And your grandfather?'

'Pappouli wasn't happy either. He left Greece and his extended family to better himself. Everyone saw me as going backwards when I dropped out of uni and started work behind a bar. It didn't count that it was at the most fashionable nightclub in Sydney at the time. No one thought it was worth applauding when I became the club's youngest ever manager. I continued to be a great disappointment.'

She knew some of this story. But not the personal insights about his family. Not how his spur to success was proving himself to them. 'If I remember, your grandfather became ill.'

'He had a stroke. I insisted on running the restaurant for him while he was in hospital. Straight away I could see Athina's time was past. It was now in the wrong end of town for a traditional Greek restaurant. The older people who had come for the nostalgia were dying off. The younger punters had moved on. I saw what could be done with it, but of course my hands were tied.'

'Until…' Dell found she couldn't say the words.

'Until my grandfather died and left the restaurant to me. You know the rest.'

Not quite all the rest—much as she ached to know it. But Alex was her boss. Knowing this was relevant to the naming of the resort. His private life continued to be none of her business. 'I see why you want to honour your grandfather. Thank you for sharing that with me.'

She'd believed she and Alex were poles apart. Perhaps they had more in common than she could have dreamed. Both brought up by parents who wanted to impose their ambitions and expectations on their kids. She'd fought those expectations to get where she was. As a result, she remained a disappointment to her parents too. Alex's arrogance and ruthlessness seemed more understandable now. But it seemed he'd paid a price.

She had to fight an impulse to hug him.

'Now I better understand your attitude in court,' she said. Not that she was condoning it.

He sighed. 'It seems a long time ago in a different place. I'm a different person.'

Was he truly? Was she? She remembered how she'd wondered if he'd worn his public image like a mask. Was she now seeing glimpses of the man behind the mask? Because she liked what she saw.

'I'd rather put it right behind me if we're to work in harmony together,' she said. *In harmony.* She was already using the language that would define this place.

'I've apologised and I hope you have forgiven me,' he said, a little stiffly. 'One day I'll take you to my family's Taverna Athina and you can see where it all started.'

'I'd like that very much.' She realised she was hungry to find out as much as possible about this man who was beginning to take up way too much time in her thoughts.

CHAPTER SEVEN

Two weeks into her new job and Dell was loving every minute of it. She and Alex worked so well together she found herself musing that if they had met under different circumstances they might be friends. *More than friends,* her insistent libido reminded her with inconvenient frequency.

Often when she was with him, from nowhere would come a flash of awareness of how heart-thuddingly handsome she found him. When he laughed—and he seemed to laugh more often these days—he threw back his head and there was a hollow in his tanned neck that she felt an insane urge to press her lips against. When they were going through a document or a set of plans, she'd become mesmerised by his hands, imagining how his long, strong fingers might feel on her bare skin.

She treasured the day he'd taken her to Athens for work. The music he'd played in the car on the way to the airport had been the same music she liked. They'd operated with the designers and suppliers like a team—so much so the people thought they'd been working together for years. But on the journey home, when she'd felt overwhelmed by sudden tiredness, she'd been very careful to stay on her side of the car. She didn't trust herself. Sometimes she'd awoken from dreams of him—dreams filled with erotic fantasy.

Every time she realised the way her thoughts were taking her, her redhead's skin would flush. She prayed he didn't notice, because she never saw anything in his reactions to her to indicate *he* might feel in any way the same about *her*.

Although he had never mentioned Mia—not once—she got the impression she'd been the love of his life and no other woman would ever measure up to her.

According to his aunt Penelope, her landlady, there was no woman in his life. Not that Dell had indulged in gossip with her about her nephew, in spite of her curiosity. There was no guarantee it wouldn't reach Alex and she doubted he'd be happy about her speculating on his love life— or lack of it—with his family. Then there was the annoying fact that Aunt Penelope appeared convinced that she and Alex were more than boss and employee. The older woman seemed to think that the more often she subtly mentioned her suspicions, the more likely Dell would cave in and admit it through the course of the conversation.

But no matter how Dell denied it, she could no longer deny the truth to herself—*she was developing a crush on her boss*.

What a cliché—and not one she had thought she would ever find herself caught up in. The anticipation of seeing him brought a frisson of unexpected pleasure to her working day. She found herself taking greater care with the way she dressed. If Alex happened to compliment her on her dress, she would hug the knowledge to herself and make sure she wore something similar the next day. He'd mentioned he liked her perfume—and she had to fight the temptation to douse herself in it. But her secret crush was harmless, she told herself. He would never know.

There was only one flaw in her new life in this Greek paradise—a new susceptibility to seasickness. It was most inconvenient when she was working on an island accessible only by boat.

Every day, Alex's cousin Cristos took her and some of the tradespeople across and back to Kosmimo in his blue-painted converted wooden fishing boat. At first she'd looked forward to it. She'd always been fine on the water, whether sailing on Sydney Harbour with friends or a cruise to Fiji with her parents.

Yet this small boat chugging across calm, clear waters had her gagging with nausea all the way. She'd sat by turns at the front and back of the boat but it was no use. In desperation, she'd got up earlier to catch the construction company's much bigger boat, but it was no different. She had to deal with a niggling nausea until mid-morning. By mid-afternoon she was dreading the return trip for another dose.

It was getting worse. This morning she'd managed to get up the steps from the jetty to the lower levels of the building and into the bath-room just in time. She'd tried eating a bigger breakfast, a smaller breakfast, no breakfast at all, but the outcome was the same.

Afterwards, she splashed cold water on her face. Fixed her make-up to try and conceal the unflattering tinge of green of her skin and brushed back her lank hair from her face. She gripped the edge of the hand basin and prac-tised her fluffy-chick smile in the mirror. The last thing she wanted was for Alex to notice all was not well.

She loved working here with him. However she was aware it was early days yet. Theoreti-cally, she was still on probation although he had told her several times how pleased he was with her job performance. But how could she continue in a job on an island only accessible by boat if she was going to feel like this every day?

Alex finished going through some plans with the plumber who was installing the fittings in the guest bathrooms. A smile of anticipation tugged at the edges of his mouth as he headed back to the office that would become the hotel's administration centre but right now served just for him and Dell. She should be at her desk by now.

He realised the day didn't really start for him until she smiled a 'good morning' greeting. Her warm presence was like the dark Greek coffee that kick-started his day. How had he managed without her?

But as he got to the office he stopped, alarmed. She was leaning on her elbows on the desk, her head resting in her hands in a pose of utter exhaustion. Had she been out last night partying late in the nightclubs of Nidri? Somehow he didn't think so. She wouldn't be so unprofessional to come to work with a hangover.

'Dell, are you okay?'

She looked up, her splayed hands still holding onto her head. 'Alex. I thought you were out the back with the builders,' she said in a voice so shaky it hardly sounded like her. Her face was so pale a smattering of freckles stood out across the bridge of her nose. Make-up was smeared around her eyes. Her wavering smile seemed forced.

'What's wrong?' he asked, fear stabbing him.

He'd become accustomed to her presence in his day. Her smile, her energy, her awesome attitude to work, the way he could fire ideas off her and she'd come back with ideas to counter or complement his own. Whatever he'd directed her to do she'd taken a step further. He'd found himself thanking whatever lucky star had made him turn around to see her in that yoga class. She couldn't be ill. Especially with so much still to do before the hotel would be ready to open. He depended on her. He couldn't imagine his days on the island without his right-hand person. Fate had delivered her to him at just the right time.

He could see what an effort it was for her to

force out the words. 'I feel dreadful. The boat. I'm getting seasick. I don't know why as I don't usually suffer from it.'

He frowned. 'But the sea is so calm.'

'I know. The first few days I was fine. But since then it's getting worse.'

'Is Cristos showing off and speeding around? That would make anyone sick.' He'd have words with his cousin if that was the case.

'Not at all, he's very good and taking extra care since I told him I wasn't feeling well.'

Maybe it was her time of the month. Alex knew enough not to suggest it. Two older sisters had trained him well in that regard. Not that he wanted to press for details. 'Are you sure it's the boat? You're living in a new country. It could be the water. Or the food. Maybe you're allergic to something. Eggplant perhaps. You told me you're on a mission to try all the different Greek ways of cooking it and put them on your blog. You could be eating too much.'

'I suppose it could be that.' She looked doubtful.

'Or a stomach flu?'

'I don't think so. But I guess it's a possibility.'

'Then I suggest you go see a doctor as soon as you can. Perhaps you need to get medication for motion sickness. At least until you get more used to the boat. Aunt Penelope will be able to help find an English-speaking doctor in Nidri. I'll take you back in my boat now.' The sooner she sorted this out, the better.

She groaned and put up her hand in protest. 'Thank you but no. I couldn't face getting back into a boat right now. I'll feel better as the day goes on and go back with Cristos this evening as usual.'

'See a doctor tomorrow. I insist. Call and make an appointment this morning. Don't come in to work until you find out what's wrong. If it's serious and you have to take time off work let me know. Whatever the result let me know.'

It was on the tip of his tongue to ask her would she like him to come with her. But that would be overstepping the mark as her employer. It would be appropriate as a friend, and he realised he already thought of her as a friend. The informal nature of their work arrangement had seen a kind of intimacy develop very quickly between them.

If he was honest with himself, he would admit he didn't view her in just a platonic way. He found her very attractive. Not his tall and blonde type, but alluring just the same. Curvy and auburn-haired was growing on him in a major way. He reacted to the sway of her hips in a tight pencil skirt, the tantalising hint of cleavage when she was shoulder to shoulder with him discussing a plan, the wide curves of her mouth. And he delighted in that smile. Always her warm, embracing smile that made him feel better than any other stimulant ever had.

But he forced himself to turn away, to switch off his feelings. He was not ready for another woman in his life. Was not certain he would *ever* be ready. And it was never a good idea to have an affair with a member of his staff.

Next morning, Dell stared across the desk at the doctor, too shocked to comprehend what she was saying. It wasn't the doctor's lightly accented

English that was incomprehensible, it was her words. 'You are pregnant, Ms Hudson.'

'You are pregnant.' The three words she had longed almost beyond reason to hear reverberated through her head but the doctor might as well have said them in Greek for all the sense they made. The middle-aged woman had insisted on Dell taking a pregnancy test, routine in cases of unexplained nausea she had said. Dell had muttered to herself about what a waste of time it was. To her utter shock, the test had proved positive. Then the doctor had examined her to confirm the diagnosis.

'But it's impossible for me to be pregnant,' Dell protested. As she explained her history, the doctor took notes.

'I would say that your IVF has been successful,' the doctor said. 'Bleeding in pregnancy is not uncommon. What you experienced could have been caused by implantation or any number of reasons. Have you had other symptoms?'

How Dell had prayed for the symptoms of pregnancy throughout all those years of hoping.

Now she was so deeply immersed in her new life she hadn't actually recognised them. The 'seasickness' that was actually morning sickness. The sensitivity of her breasts she'd put down to the havoc IVF had played with her hormones. The tiredness she'd attributed to the long hours in her new job.

'I believe so,' she said slowly, then explained her symptoms to the doctor.

'I'm sure a blood test will confirm your pregnancy,' the doctor said. 'Congratulations.'

Dell's head was reeling. It was too much to take in. This was the best and the worst of news. *A baby at last.* But pregnant by IVF to her ex-husband while she was living in a different country on the other side of the world from home and with a halfway serious crush on another man?

Through a haze of disbelief, she made a further appointment with the doctor. Then walked blindly out into the street.

Nidri was more a boisterous, overgrown village than a town. Dell tripped on the uneven pavement and gave a hysterical little laugh that had a well-dressed woman turn and look at her askance. She steadied herself against the wall of a beauty salon that specialised in tiny fish nibbling the dead skin from people's feet. Moved on to a *fournos* with a tempting display of the most delicious local cookies and pastries. In her shocked, nauseated state the scent of baking did not appeal.

She was struggling to find a foothold in the suddenly turned upside down landscape of her own life. She would have to take step by dazed step to try to negotiate the uncharted new territory. Not at all certain where it would lead her.

Alex. How would she tell him? What would this mean? Almost certainly the end of her dream job. The end of the already remote chance that they could ever be more than friends. She wrapped her arms tightly around herself against the shivers that shuddered through her, even though the warm spring sun shone down on her shoulders.

CHAPTER EIGHT

ALL NIGHT ALEX had been plagued by a nagging concern for Dell. He'd become so concerned that next morning he decided to take his boat across to Nidri so he could check on her. Her ailment had sounded like something more than seasickness. What if she was seriously ill?

His gut clenched at the thought. Dell had become his responsibility. He had talked her into moving to Greece to work with him even though she had been initially reluctant. Now it was up to him to look out for her. He was all she had here. The job had kept her way too busy for her to get out and make friends. He hoped the doctor's diagnosis would be something easily fixed. That *he* could fix for her.

His aunt Penelope had pointed him in the direction to where Dell was seeing the doctor. He stood across the road and waited for her to come out of her appointment. It wasn't a long wait. He caught sight of her immediately, in the short pencil skirt he liked so much and a crisp striped shirt—she had obviously intended to head to work afterwards. Cristos was on call to take her over.

But as he watched her walk away from the doctor's rooms, Alex wished he'd been somewhere closer. *What the hell was wrong?* She seemed to lurch as if in a daze, tripping on the uneven pavement, righting herself without seeming to realise what she was doing. Finally she stood out of the way in the doorway of a closed souvenir shop and hugged her arms tightly around herself. Her hair shone bright in a shaft of sunlight. Had she been prescribed medication? Was she suffering from a fever? Been given bad news? *She should not be on her own.*

He broke into a run to get to her. Cursing the traffic, he ducked in and out of cars and buses. The delivery guy on a bicycle balancing an enormous flower arrangement shouted at him but he scarcely heard him. *He had to reach her.* 'Dell!'

She looked up, seemed to have trouble focusing, her eyes huge in her wan face, her lovely mouth trembling. Alex was struck by how vulnerable and alone she seemed. How suddenly *frail*.

He felt swept by an almighty urge to protect her, to make her safe. An urge that went beyond the concern of an employer for a member of staff. *He cared for her.* Alex didn't know when or how it had happened, but somehow she had snuck under his defences. All he knew was he wanted to fold her into his arms and tell her everything would be all right because he was there for her.

'Alex,' she said. 'Wh...what are you doing here?' Her eyes darted every which way. As if she'd rather be anywhere but with him right at this moment. As if she was looking for an escape route, not a pair of comforting arms. Especially not *his*.

Alex shoved his hands into his pockets. He

forced his voice to calm, boss-like concern. 'To see if you're all right. Which you're obviously not. What news from the doctor?'

Emotions that he couldn't read flickered across her face. *Secrets she didn't want to share.* People shouldered past them on the narrow pavement. An English couple standing outside a shop loudly discussed the benefits of olive wood salad servers. Motor scooters in dire need of adjustment to their exhaust systems puttered by. 'Can we maybe go somewhere more private?' she said, her voice so low he could scarcely catch it.

'There's a coffee shop just up there,' he said, indicating it with a wave of his arm. 'You look like you could do with Greek coffee, hot and strong.' If it weren't only mid-morning he'd suggest brandy.

She shuddered and swallowed hard. 'Some orange juice, I think.'

'Sure,' he said. 'Whatever you need.' He put his arm around her shoulder to shepherd her in the right direction. Initially she stiffened against his touch, then the rigidity of her body melted.

Her curves felt soft and warm against him. Alex tightened his hold to keep her close, liking the feeling he could keep her safe. But as soon as they reached the coffee shop she broke away from him.

He sat her down at a table in a quiet corner. Pushed the juice towards her. Once she'd taken a few sips, she seemed to revive somewhat, although there was still a worrying pallor to her face.

'Thank you,' she said. Her hands cradled around the glass in an effort, he realised, to stop their trembling.

'So what's wrong? Eggplant allergy?'

A hint of a smile—perhaps ten per cent of its full incandescent power—hovered around the corners of her mouth. 'Not quite,' she said. She met his gaze directly. 'There's no easy way to say this. Turns out the seasickness wasn't that at all. I…I'm pregnant.' She sounded as though she didn't quite believe it, was just trying on the words for size.

Alex reeled back in his chair, too stunned to

say anything. Shock at her words mingled with his own disbelief and disappointment. And a sudden bolt of jealousy that she had a man in her life. A man she had denied. 'Did you know about this when you accepted the job with me?'

The words spilled out from her. As if she was trying to explain the situation to herself as well as to him. 'No. It came as a complete shock. I… I thought—hoped—there was a chance, which is why I said no to your offer in the first place. Then…well, then it seemed I wasn't pregnant. But…the evidence that led me to think I wasn't pregnant and could accept your job turned out to be a false alarm. Turns out, though, I am pregnant.'

'You said you didn't have a man in your life. "One hundred per cent single," if I remember correctly.'

'I don't. There hasn't been anyone for a long time.'

He drummed his fingers on the metal top of the table. 'That doesn't make sense.'

'I realise that. It…it's complicated.'

Cynicism welled up and spouted into his words. 'What's complicated about getting a woman pregnant?' He didn't know why his reaction to her news was so sour. Perhaps because he'd started to think of Dell as *his*. Her news made it very clear she had another man in her life. *The father of her child.*

'We all know how it happens.' Had she met a man since she'd been in Greece? One of his family? His cousin? She'd remarked on several occasions how good-looking Cristos was. He had no right to be furious if that was the case, he had no claim on her, but a black rage consumed him at the thought.

She bit her lower lip. 'In this case, not quite the way you think,' she said with a dull edge to her voice.

'Perhaps you'd better explain.' He made no effort to keep his disillusionment from his voice. One of the things he'd liked most about her was her open face, her apparent honesty. It appeared he'd read her incorrectly.

* * *

Dell quailed against Alex's grim expression. He hadn't been able to hide his shock at her revelation. Of course he'd be annoyed, angry even that his newly contracted employee was pregnant. It had been an incredible shock to her, too. But her joy in finally seeing her dream of motherhood in sight overrode everything.

There was no point in telling him anything other than the unembellished truth. She took a steadying breath. 'This baby was conceived by IVF. I'd been undergoing treatment during my marriage.'

Alex's dark brows pulled into an even deeper frown. 'But you're divorced now.'

'Yes,' she said. 'Legally divorced. The marriage is done and dusted.'

'So who is the father?'

'My ex-husband.'

He pushed back in his chair. Slanted his shoulders away from her. It hurt to see him distancing himself. 'I don't get it,' he said.

Dell caught a half-sob in her throat. She'd

known this wouldn't be easy. But she hadn't expected it would be this difficult. 'The IVF procedures I had when I was married to Neil didn't work. It was one of the reasons we broke up. Well, not broke up strictly speaking. He left me. I hadn't been expecting it. But he wanted out. He blamed my obsession with having a baby and… and for neglecting him as a husband.'

Alex's eyes narrowed. 'And was that the reason?'

'Looking back, I see it did put the marriage under stress. I always thought having a baby was what we both wanted. But maybe…maybe it was more about me. I'd always wanted to have kids, felt a failure that I couldn't fall pregnant when everyone around me seemed to do it so easily. My life became a roller coaster of alternate anticipation then despair. And with some hormone crazy happening too. Maybe there were cracks in the marriage I just didn't want to see. That it wasn't strong enough to survive the pressure.'

She looked down at her hands, realised abstractedly that the dent from where she'd worn her wedding ring for so long had finally disappeared.

Alex shifted in his chair, obviously uncomfortable. She appreciated this was an awkwardly personal conversation for a boss with his employee. 'That still doesn't enlighten me to how you're pregnant to your ex-husband.'

'It took me a while to pick myself up from the aftermath of my marriage. We'd been dating since high school and—'

'So you'd been with the same guy since high school?' Alex sounded incredulous. She remembered his reputation as a player and a man about town before he'd met the lovely Mia. How tame her own life had been in comparison. But she hadn't wanted it any other way.

She nodded. 'He was nice. Steady. I thought he'd be a good husband and father.'

There hadn't been a lot of fireworks to start and what there had been had eventually fizzled out. But then it hadn't been sizzling sensuality she'd been after. She'd seen Neil as steady and secure and a family man totally unlike her distant father. Had it been enough? For the first time she wondered if sex had become the effort for Neil that it had for her. It had become all about making babies, not making love. She thought about the thrill she felt just being in the same room as Alex. Had she ever felt that way about her ex-husband?

'But he didn't turn out so nice,' Alex said.

Slowly she shook her head. 'To be fair, there must have been wrong on both sides for the marriage to have ended.'

'So how did you manage on your own?'

She shrugged. 'Okay.' Of course it hadn't been okay but she didn't want to admit that to Alex. Of how Neil had screwed her out of her fair share of their assets. How she'd been left with the considerable IVF expense as he'd convinced her it was what she'd wanted, not him. She hadn't been able to understand how he'd turned so nasty until she'd discovered he'd met someone else while they were still married and had moved in with her straight away.

Alex's dark eyes were perceptive. 'Really okay?'

'Not really.' An awkward silence fell between them. But she had no desire to discuss her dating disasters with Alex. That was something she could laugh at with her girlfriends. Not with the only man who had attracted her since—well, pretty well ever.

Alex was the one to break the silence. 'So… back to your pregnancy.'

'The fertility clinic got in touch, asked me what I wanted to do with our last stored embryo.' She implored him with her eyes to understand. 'I'd wanted a baby for so long. Desperately. I saw this as my last chance. At twenty-nine I was running out of time to meet a guy who wanted to get married and have kids. Start again. I told the clinic I wanted to try.'

'What did your ex say?'

Dell found it difficult to meet Alex's eyes. Concentrated instead on the pattern of olives printed on the café placemat. 'Here's where it gets complicated. I didn't tell him.'

'What?' His voice made no bones about his disapproval. 'You didn't tell the guy who fathered it?'

She looked up at him again. There was no point in dissembling. 'I know. It was probably wrong. Even immoral.' She leaned over the table towards him. 'But you don't understand what baby hunger feels like. A constant ache. Torture every time you see someone else's baby. When you have to congratulate a friend who's pregnant and all the time you're screaming inside *why not me?*'

'No. I don't understand that,' he said shortly.

'Don't judge me, Alex. I did what I did because I had to grab that one, final chance of achieving the dream of holding my baby in my arms. I didn't hold out any hopes as no attempt had ever worked before. But when the chance was offered to me I had no choice but to take it.'

'Is that why you initially turned down my job offer?'

'Yes. I didn't want to be away from home if by some miracle the treatment worked. It never had before but I kept alive that tiny beam of hope. Until…until it appeared I had failed again. Evidence that it turns out was false.'

'So what does your ex think of this?'

'What? Me being pregnant? I only just found out myself. He doesn't know.'

'When do you intend to tell him?' It was ironic, she thought, that she had told Alex, her boss, before the biological father.

'Not…not yet. The pregnancy is still in its early stages. I…I…may still lose it. I wouldn't want to tell him until I'm more sure. Why go through all that for nothing?'

'You obviously don't anticipate a happy reaction.' Alex's fingers drummed on the table top. Dell resisted the temptation to reach over and still them with her own.

'He's moved on. Married already to the woman he left me for.' Swift, brutal, her ex had put their years together behind him as if they'd never happened.

She'd made the decision to take the embryo without really thinking about Neil. Possibly she'd even justified it by remembering how he'd said she wanted the IVF so much, she could pay the bills for it. Didn't that make the baby hers and hers alone? In her heart she knew that thinking was wrong. Not so much for Neil's sake—though she knew he had a right to know he was going to be a father—but for the baby's sake. Her child deserved to know about his or her other parent. The idea of a baby had seemed so abstract. Now it was beginning to feel real. A little person she hoped she would be bringing into the world. And for whom she bore the entire responsibility. It was both terrifying and exhilarating.

'What do you intend to do?'

'Give you my resignation, along with my sincere apology, if that's what you want. I certainly don't blame you if you do.'

He leaned forward across the table. 'Is that what you want? Legally, I can't fire an employee for being pregnant.' For a moment she saw a flash of her old adversary in the set of his jaw.

'It wouldn't come to that,' she said. 'I...I...'

She was going to say *I love working with you* but somehow she couldn't utter the word *love* to him under any circumstance. Not with the knowledge of her secret crush on him throbbing away in her heart. 'I really enjoy working with you and would like to continue. The baby isn't due until after Christmas. I would like to stay here and help you with the launch, then return to Australia at the end of summer, say late August. I need to be back there for the birth.'

He leaned back against the chair. Templed his fingers. 'You're sure you want to do that?'

'Yes. I really want to continue working with you. To…to be part of your awesome project.' *To stay part of his life.*

His expression didn't give away anything. She had no idea what his decision would be. She would accept it either way. But she just hoped he would agree to keep her on.

'With all the hospitality staff I've employed over the years, I've worked with pregnant women. There's no reason not to keep you on.'

Hope bubbled through her. 'You mean I've still got a job?'

'Yes,' he said.

'You're not just saying that because you'd be breaking some employment code if you asked me to go?'

'No,' he said gruffly. 'I want you to stay. I consider you an…an indispensable part of my team.'

She wanted to fling her arms around his neck to thank him, but knew it would be totally inappropriate. Especially now considering her condition.

'Thank you,' she said. 'I promise I won't let you down.'

'What about your motion sickness?'

'The doctor has given me some strategies to cope with that,' she said. 'No medication, of course.'

'What about the boat ride to and from the island every day? You looked very shaken by it yesterday.'

Her chin tilted up. She wouldn't give him any excuse to renege on his decision. 'I'll just have to grit my teeth and bear it, won't I?' she said. 'This job is really important to me, Alex.' *You are important to me, but I'll never be able to let you know that now.*

'I think there's a better way. You should move onto the island.'

'But…but none of the rooms are ready for occupation,' she said.

'There are two self-contained suites in the pavilion,' he said. 'You'll have to share it with me.'

CHAPTER NINE

HOW DID SHE deal with this new development?

Sharing an apartment with Alex would be quite the challenge, Dell realised. That afternoon, she followed him as he carried her suitcase across the marble floor of the pavilion into the sumptuous bedroom that was to be hers. She noted that, as he had said, the bedrooms and bathrooms were completely separate—thank heaven.

Growing up, she had shared a bathroom with her brother. And of course she had shared a bathroom with her ex. But she could not even imagine having to share a bathroom with Alex. Not in a room where the occupants spent most of their time naked. Not when her imagination would go crazy thinking about him naked in the same space where *she* was naked. Standing where he stood to shower that tall, broad-shouldered body, twisting to soap his powerful chest and lean, six-pack belly. At least, she assumed he'd have a six-pack belly. He did in those dreams that came to taunt and tantalise her—where he was wearing considerably fewer clothes than he did in real life. She shook her head to clear her thoughts. *Enough.*

She had to stop this crazy fantasising about Alex. It was never going to happen. She was pregnant and he was *not* okay with it, no matter how much he quoted his employer code of practice. Her pregnancy was an inconvenience to him. There'd never before been a sign he was interested in her as anything other than an employee; there certainly wouldn't be now she was pregnant. She had a thrilling new life ahead of her—mother to her miracle baby—and that life would not include Alex. Once she went back to Australia she doubted he would be anything more than a name on her résumé, her boss on a particularly exciting project.

That new life was not quite the way she had

envisaged it for all those years—having the child's father around had been the plan. But she had not the slightest regret about her rash visit to the clinic. In fact the more she thought about it, the happier she became that she had made that reckless choice. *Her baby.* Now she needed to concentrate on doing the best possible job she could do so Alex would not regret keeping her on in a job she still sorely needed. She needed to earn to both pay off her debts and start saving for the baby. Indulging in fantasies about her handsome boss was a time-wasting distraction.

'This bedroom is magnificent,' she said, looking around her at the restful, white room straight out of a glossy interiors magazine. The furniture was sleek and modern, the huge bed piled with expensive linens and pillows. A few carefully chosen paintings hung on the walls, contemporary works she recognised as being by the artist she had visited in Athens with Alex. He had commissioned a series of arresting scenes of the islands for the resort. Nature also provided its own artworks, the windows framed a view of the green hills behind. Tasteful. Private. Peaceful. Well, as peaceful as it could be with *him* in a room just across a corridor. 'It's incredibly luxurious for a pool house,' she said.

'I understand the previous owner lived in it when he flew in to check on the construction of the main house.'

'That makes sense,' she said. 'Is your room the same as this one?'

Why did she say that? She didn't want him to show her his bedroom. To see his bed and imagine him there, his tanned, olive skin against the pale linen sheets, as he sprawled across— She flushed that tell-tale flush but thankfully he still had his back to her. Why was her libido leading her on such a dance? Pregnancy hormones? Or *him*? She didn't need to think about the answer. Fight the unwelcome feeling as she might, she had never felt so attracted to a man.

'Yeah, it's the same,' he said. 'A slightly different colour scheme.' He was more subdued than she'd seen him, closed off, communicating only what he needed to. Possibly he was regretting his offer for her to share the pavilion with him.

What would he think if he could see the scenarios playing in her head, where he played a starring role? Again she flushed, this time with mortification.

She forced herself back to the real world. He was her boss. She was nothing more to him than an employee—valued, she knew, but an underling just the same. Now she felt she had to work even harder, to prove herself to him all over again. Prove that being pregnant was no barrier to performance. She would do well to keep reminding herself of that.

'Thank you, Alex, for this. I think I feel better already knowing I don't have to face that boat trip twice a day. As soon as the sickness abates I can go back to the villa.'

'When you're ready,' he said. 'You can stay here as long as you need to.'

Dell followed him through to the spacious living area and kitchen. Despite her good working relationship with Alex, she felt awkward at the subtle shift between them that being room-mates would inevitably bring. She knew she was intruding but at the same time she was very grateful for the offer of such wonderful accommodation on the island. She was happy at the villa but this apartment was the ultimate in opulence. Once the resort was up and going, the pavilion would become exclusive, highly priced accommodation for well-heeled guests. What a treat to stay here in the meantime. She could never afford this level of luxury on her own dime.

'So how do we handle this?' she asked him. 'I'm aware I'm invading your privacy and I'll stay out of your way as much as possible. What do you do about food? Do you cook for yourself or—?' She actually knew a daily housekeeper came over on the construction crew boat every day to cook and clean for him. But she didn't want to admit she'd been snooping into his life.

He told her what she already knew and she pretended it was news to her. 'The housekeeper can leave meals for you, too, if you like,' he said. 'Or you can order what you need to cook your own meals. Just coordinate with her when you're likely to need to use the kitchen. There's breakfast stuff in the pantry. Again, order what you need.'

So no shared meals, then. No intimate evenings over the elegant table set in the loggia overlooking the pool. Not that she'd expected that. Alex made it very clear he put her in the same category as the housekeeper—mere staff.

'I'll leave you to unpack and settle in,' he said. 'Then you can join me in the office. That is, if you feel up to it.' He was bending over backwards to be considerate when she knew he must be cursing the break in their timetable.

'I'm feeling better by the minute, just knowing I don't have to get back into a boat every day.'

He paused. 'I need to go to Athens again day after tomorrow. Will you be able to come?'

'I'll manage,' she said. 'I don't want to miss out.' If she had to nibble on dry crackers and swig lemonade all day to keep the nausea at bay she'd be there.

'We'll have a very full day. Pack for a night away,' he said. 'If you want to see the Acropolis, it might be a good opportunity to get up early and do it before we fly back. I don't know how you'll feel about all the walking and steps involved in getting up to the Parthenon once you're further into your pregnancy. It will get too hot as well.'

'That's very thoughtful of you. I'd love to.' *Why was he being so nice?*

'Good.' He turned on his heel. 'I'll see you in the office. I've got work to catch up on.' The implication being he had lost valuable time attending to her. Dell felt bad about that. She had hours to make up too. She'd work later that evening. Which would make any awkward encounters in the pool house less likely. She would be careful to schedule her meals around his so she did not intrude.

He started to stride away. 'Alex. Before you go. One more thing.'

He turned back to face her.

'Your aunt Penelope…'

'Yes?'

'I got to like her while I was staying in the villa. She's teaching me Greek, you know. And sharing her traditional recipes. My blog fans are loving them.'

'Very nice,' he said dismissively. But Dell felt she had to plough on.

'As I got to know her, I realised that she…well, your aunt Penelope is the disseminator of information to your extended family.'

'Which is your kind way of saying she's an outrageous gossip.'

Dell laughed. 'I wouldn't quite say it like that, but yes.'

Alex laughed too and Dell felt a relaxing of the thread of tension that had become so taut between them since she'd dropped her bombshell back at the café in Nidri.

He might not be so relaxed when he heard what she had to say next. 'Er…with that in mind, do you realise your aunt thinks I'm moving in to the pool house to be with you? I mean, not to share like a roommate, to actually live with you. She's convinced we're lovers.'

'What?' Alex exploded. 'Where the hell did she get that idea from?' His eyes narrowed. 'What did you say to give her that opinion?'

'Nothing. Not a word, I promise you. As far as I'm concerned you're the boss and I'm the employee. You're helping me out because I'm suffering so much from motion sickness it's affecting my efficiency in my job. That's all I told her.'

His face set granite hard. 'It needs to be perfectly clear that there is nothing else whatsoever between us and never could be.' Dell tried not to react to the shard of pain that speared her at his words. She knew that to be the case, but hearing it so vehemently expressed hurt.

'*Promnestria.*' He spat the Greek word.

'What does that mean?' Dell asked. 'It…er… doesn't sound very pleasant.'

'It means "matchmaker", and I'm using it as a shortcut to express how annoyed I am at the interference from my family—well-meaning as they are. My aunt, and some of the other women, know very well I don't intend ever to marry. Yet they continue to speculate about me and every halfway eligible female who comes my way. And even the entirely unsuitable ones.'

Like me, thought Dell, the shard of pain stabbing deeper.

He cursed some more under his breath. This time she didn't ask for a translation.

'I'm afraid there's more,' she said.

He rolled his eyes heavenward. 'I'm so fond of my aunt but—'

'She also suspects I'm pregnant. I think she recognised the signs I never saw myself. At her age I guess she's seen it all before. I have a feeling she's crowing with delight because she thinks my baby is…is, well, yours.'

The normally eloquent Alex seemed completely lost for words. Dell squirmed in an agony of expectation of his reaction. Suddenly her job didn't seem so secure after all.

When he finally found his voice, it was ominously calm. 'How on earth would she think that?'

Dell shrugged. 'I guess she thought we knew each other in Australia. Put two and two together and came up with completely the wrong answer.'

'What have you told her?' Again she caught a glimpse of her old adversary. Alex seemed as though he was looking for her to slip up in her evidence. Had he really changed? She so wanted to believe he had.

She willed him to believe she was telling the truth. 'Nothing, I assure you. Not about the court case, nothing. I'm here to work, Alex, not to gossip with your family. I mean it.' It was a trap she'd been determined not to fall into, beguiling as Aunt Penelope could be.

'Good,' he said abruptly. But his taut look relaxed and she felt like she was off the witness stand.

'It won't be long before it becomes obvious

that I'm pregnant. Should I tell your aunt? And that the baby isn't yours?'

He shook his head. 'My publicity director's personal life is none of their concern. Although in one way you telling them would quell some of the speculation about the reason you've moved in here. People close to me know I would never get involved with a woman carrying another man's child.'

His eyes didn't meet hers as he said that. Dell was relieved. It gave her valuable seconds to hide her surprise. Was that a message for her? She didn't need it spelled out.

'On balance,' he continued, 'your pregnancy is your business. My family can stay out of it.' Not for one moment would he think she might not want him along.

'I shall hereby resist all hints, innuendos and subtly worded questions,' she said, holding up her hand as if swearing an oath.

'Thank you,' he said. He stilled, his shoulders tensed, his stance braced. 'I can't bear to be the subject of gossip—my private life bandied around as if it's some game. Not after…not after everything that happened. When I couldn't turn around without seeing a paparazzi shot of myself with some journalist analysing my expression and suggesting what I was feeling. Photos of her and me together before…before…' His words faltered to an end in a tortured groan.

Again Dell felt a great rush of compassion for him. She couldn't begin to imagine how she would have dealt with what he had been through, the horror and loss, the immeasurable pain. She ached to put her arms around him and comfort him. But he was her boss and she his employee and he had drawn the line between them. She kept her distance.

'I promise I will not encourage your aunt in any speculation about my personal life or yours. Not that I will be seeing much of her while I'm staying on the island. There's a lot to be done here. I'm going to concentrate my efforts on that.'

'As far as my family is concerned, I suggest we present a united front—your role in helping me with the launch of Pevezzo Athina is why we spend time together,' he said. 'There is nothing else of interest to great-aunts, aunts, cousins and whoever else seems determined to see something else that simply isn't there.'

His tone was businesslike in the extreme, in complete denial of the informal, friendly tone she had become used to. As he spoke, she noticed the shift in the angle of his shoulders away from her, distancing her, re-establishing boundaries.

'Of course,' she said, swallowing against the lump of disappointment that threatened to choke her.

He turned on his heel to head out of the pavilion and towards the main building.

Dell watched him, his stride both powerful and graceful as he walked away, each footstep seeming to determine a new distance between them.

Some of the magic of this special place where she had been so happy seemed to spiral away above him to dissipate in the cloudless blue sky.

CHAPTER TEN

TWO DAYS LATER Alex gritted his teeth as he walked by Dell's bedroom suite. From behind the closed door he could hear the faint splashing of her shower. He could plug his ears to the sound. But he couldn't block his imagination. Images bombarded him of her in there, naked, the water flowing over the creamy skin of her shoulders, her breasts and downwards over the curves of her hips. Was she slowly soaping her body? Did she have her face tilted up towards the jets of water as if she was preparing to receive a kiss?

His kiss.

His wild imaginings were torture. Living with Dell in such close proximity was torture. Even a glass left on the sink with the lipstick outline of her lips on the rim drove him into a frenzy of fantasising about that mouth on his. It was crazy. And totally unlike him.

He'd always been confident with women. To be frank, he'd never had to chase them. From the age of fourteen they'd chased him. And he'd been only too happy to be caught. He'd never gone through that stage of stuttering awkwardness in the presence of a beautiful woman. Until now.

The pressure of denying his attraction to his lovely employee, totally out of bounds because she was pregnant to another man, was telling on him. To his immense frustration, conversation with her about anything other than work had become awkward, stilted. *Because of him.*

He could tell she was puzzled at his often abrupt tone, at his silences. She made the effort to be her usual friendly self, but with an edge of uncertainty as she became unsure of his reaction. But he seemed incapable of returning to that comfortable working relationship, that easy camaraderie and repartee. Not when he couldn't get her out of his thoughts. Not as a trusted workmate. Or a person he thought could be a friend. But a smart, sensual, very appealing woman. A woman he *desired.*

He wasn't looking for this. He didn't want it. Not when her pregnancy complicated everything. But the feeling wouldn't go away. No matter how many times he plunged into the chilly water of the pool and swam laps until he was exhausted.

When she'd lived at the villa, he could escape to the pavilion. Now her warm presence had invaded his man cave, where he'd been able to retreat with his dark thoughts and memories. In just days, it had become stamped with her personality, even when she wasn't actually there. The sound of her laughter seemed to linger on the empty stillness, tantalising hints of her perfume wafted to greet him, there was Dell food in the fridge.

The enforced intimacy was making him yearn for something more, needs and feelings he had long denied himself because of the guilt that tore him apart over Mia's death. Sharing a house with a woman—if only in the roommate sense—was bringing back painful memories of his late fiancée.

He had been happy dating Mia but she had pressed for more commitment. In fact she had delivered an ultimatum—get engaged or she walked. He had agreed to the engagement, she had agreed to move in. But then it had stalled with his ambivalence about setting a date for the wedding. As their relationship had gone on, he hadn't been certain they had enough in common to build a life together, the kind of committed family life he'd had growing up with his parents and grandparents. Under his playboy, party prince exterior that was what he'd known he'd wanted one day. He still hadn't been certain Mia was the one when he'd sent her to her death.

Dell was so different, in looks, personality, everything. Put both women together and Dell would be overshadowed by Mia's tall, model-perfect looks. He couldn't, *wouldn't* compare them. Yet in his mind he could almost see Dell looking up at the other woman with a wry smile, unleashing her own vibrant beauty in acknowledging Mia's statuesque Scandinavian looks. And Mia would smile back. Mia would have liked her, and Dell would have liked Mia. Polar opposites they might be, but they were both warm, kind people.

Mia had connected with his wild, party animal side. Together they had worked hard and played hard. Dell… Dell was something altogether different. There was a connection with her he had never felt before, a sense of certainty, of continuity. They thought in the same way. He kept coming back to that concept of fate. It was almost as if she'd been sent to him to help redeem and heal him.

And yet it was impossible. He could not get around the fact she was pregnant to another man. Okay, so it was a 'test-tube baby'. He didn't have to torture himself with images of her making love with her ex. Of the baby being a product of an intimate union rather than a laboratory procedure.

But being in Greece only intensified an even

deeper connection—the connection to his family and heritage. In a traditional Greek family like he came from, blood was everything. Even generations down the track and in Australia, thousands of miles away from the land of his ancestors, that hadn't changed. His family had liked Mia, but he knew they would have been a whole lot happier if she too had come from a Greek migrant family.

That deeply ingrained sense of family made the concept of taking on another man's child seem alien to him. His attitude was something he couldn't change—it was as much of him as the proud Mikhalis nose that went back through generations of males in his family. He had admired Jesse Morgan for accepting Lizzie's daughter when he had married her. Jesse adored little Amy, had an amicable relationship with the little girl's French father. But taking on another man's child was something Alex could never see himself doing.

He was so lost in his thoughts he started when the door to her room opened and Dell stood in the doorway. He had to force himself not to stare. She was wrapped in a white towelling bathrobe, her hair in damp tendrils around her face, cheeks flushed from the warmth of the shower. The neckline of the robe had fallen open to reveal a hint of cleavage and the smooth top curve of her breasts. Her legs were bare. *Was she naked under there?* He balled his hands by his sides.

'Is everything okay?' she said. 'I'm not late, am I? I got up in plenty of time so we'd get the plane to Athens.'

'It's okay,' he said gruffly, looking at her feet rather than letting his gaze centre on her chest. She had small, well-shaped feet with pink-painted toenails. Lovely from top to toe, came the thought from nowhere.

She frowned. 'It's just I heard you pacing up and down and wondered if—'

'I wasn't pacing,' he said.

'You needed to see me,' she said at the same time, with a small, perplexed frown.

'No,' he said.

'You could have knocked on the door if you

did,' she said. 'I'm always there if…if you need me.' Her voice faltered away.

For a long moment their gazes met. For the first time he saw something in her green eyes that kick-started his heart into a violent thudding. An awareness, an unspoken acknowledgement that he was not alone in his feelings. That if he were to pull her into his arms and slide that robe down her shoulders, she would not object.

He took a step backward. Broke that connection with an abrupt turning away from her. 'I'll be out by the pool. Meet me there when you're ready. We've got a lot to get done in Athens.'

The next morning, Dell looked at the computer-generated images on the screen with immense interest. She and Alex were in the architect's studio in the old centre of Athens in a street behind Syntagma Square. From the get-go, Alex had involved her in every aspect of the resort, not just the food, which was her primary area of expertise, and she was fascinated by how the plans had developed.

The designer was showing them on screen realistic images of how the interiors of Pevezzo Athina would look when everything was finished and ready for guests. The images were so detailed Dell could imagine herself walking through the rooms, furnished right down to the flower arrangements on the tables and the towels in the bathrooms.

'Every detail and change we discussed last meeting is there, looking perfect.' *We*. How easily she slipped into referring to herself and Alex as *we*. 'It makes it seem so real, so close to completion.'

She straightened up and in doing so caught Alex's eye. They shared a quick smile of complicity and triumph. They were a team and their team was firing on all cylinders.

Dell felt an overwhelming sense of relief. She'd mourned the loss of the easy feeling between them back at the island. Tortured herself with the thought that maybe he'd become aware of her crush on him and had backed off in discomfort. Perhaps moving in to the pavilion had been a mistake. Living in such close proximity was only making it more difficult—she had to be continually on alert.

She thought she'd kept her feelings carefully hidden, effectively masked. Then there had been a moment yesterday morning at that post-shower encounter when she'd sworn a recognition of mutual want had flashed between them. But the shutters had come down leaving just his inscrutable expression. Had she given herself away? Had she imagined his response?

He'd hardly spoken afterwards. On the journey she had been too busy keeping the nausea at bay to be concerned at the paucity of conversation, the silences that had been anything but comfortable.

But from the first meeting the day before, things had started to ease. Perhaps it was because at their meetings the designers and suppliers treated them as a team they started to behave like one again. She used the word *team* loosely. For all the politeness, for all the acknowledgement of her role as his assistant, the deference was very much to Alex as the boss. He was the person with the money and the authority and the power—the man who owned a private island and was spending a fortune on the services these talented people were providing. While they spoke mainly in English there were times they needed to break into Greek. She listened carefully but could only identify the odd word here and there. Still, that was better than when she'd first arrived, thanks to Aunt Penelope.

'Any other thoughts on the interior design?' Alex asked her now, indicating the CGI.

She shook her head. 'If you're happy, I reckon you can sign off on it.'

'Done,' he said and they again shared a smile.

That smile warmed her. Leaving the island to fly to Athens had been a good move. It marked, she hoped, a return to the working relationship that had bonded them in the first place. In her deepest heart she longed for the impossible, but was content to have their work camaraderie back.

Hands were shaken all round, congratulations

and thanks expressed. Then she and Alex were back out of the office and into the mid-morning busy street. She looked around her avidly trying to soak in as much detail as possible—the historical buildings guarded by soldiers in fabulous traditional uniforms, the shopfronts, what people were wearing, the buzz of it all. One day she would love to spend more time here. Again that feeling of excitement swept through her that she was actually living in Greece. She needed to make the most of it before she went home to Australia. She pushed aside the feelings of sadness that looming return evoked in her. When big dreams collided there was ultimately a casualty.

'That was the last meeting for today,' Alex said. 'Time well spent. Thank you for your contribution.'

He really was a wonderful boss, certainly not the tyrant some had painted him in Sydney. Had his reputation sprung from a resentment of his high standards, envy even? Or had he really changed as he claimed to have done?

'Back to the hotel?' she asked.

After a jam-packed afternoon of meetings, they had spent the previous night in a luxurious hotel not far from Plaka, the oldest and most historical part of Athens. Separate rooms, of course, but on the same floor.

Alex had gone out to a fashionable bar and restaurant in Syntagma with one of his cousins. To her surprise, he had invited her too, though she suspected it was more from good manners than any real desire to have her along. Her presence would only fuel the rumours in his family that she was more than an employee.

But she'd been too exhausted to accept. She did not want to admit to her bone-deep tiredness as she didn't want to remind him of her pregnancy, or that it could affect her capacity to work. Rather she'd had dinner in her room, looked for a long time at the amazing view of ancient ruins lit up from below and gone to bed very early.

Now he looked at her trim business suit and medium-heeled shoes; her stilettos had been put away until after the baby was born. 'You might want to change before you climb the Acropolis.'

'There's still time before we have to leave for the airport?' The meeting had run a little late.

'Your expedition was built into the schedule.'

'I don't quite understand why you did that, but thank you,' she said, looking up at him.

He didn't meet her eyes. 'It pleases me that you like Greece so much, are learning the language. Visiting one of our most significant historical sites is to be encouraged.'

Dell thought there was rather more to it than that. Remembered he had said he wanted to make amends for the past. But she didn't want to bring up the court case again. It seemed a lifetime ago that they had been enemies.

'I can't wait,' she said. 'I've wanted to see the Parthenon since I was a kid.'

'I chose the hotel for its easy access,' he said. 'We'll make our way through Plaka up onto the Acropolis, right up to the Parthenon and the Temple of Athena.'

It took a moment for the significance of what

he'd said to sink in. *'We?'* she asked, her heart suddenly pounding. 'Are you—?'

'Coming with you? Of course.' He spoke with the confident assuredness she found so appealing.

'There's no need, you know. I'm perfectly okay by myself,' she said. Her fingers were mentally crossed that he would not agree.

'I want to come with you, Dell,' he said. His tone, to her delight, brooked no disagreement.

She knew her pleasure at the prospect of his company was beaming from her eyes but she didn't care. For just this few hours she was going to pretend there were no barriers between them and enjoy every second of her time alone with him.

CHAPTER ELEVEN

ALEX WAS GLAD he had booked a late flight back to Preveza. This was to be no cursory trip up to the Acropolis so Dell could check off a tourist 'must-see'. She stopped to examine and exclaim at everything on the walk up the rocky outcrop that towered over the city of Athens, the ancient citadel of the Acropolis that dated back to the fifth century BC. She was the one who filled him in on the dates and facts. Her knowledge of ancient Greek history was impressive, though when he complimented her, she demurred saying it was snippets she remembered from high school. Oh, and a little brushing up on the Internet.

First of the ancient structures to catch her attention was the Herodes open-air amphitheatre, with its semi-circular rows of marble seating built in tiers from the stage, built in 161 AD. 'Can you imagine how many people must have been entertained here over the centuries?' she said as, after a long pause for thoughtful contemplation, she snapped photos with her smartphone.

'And continue to do so,' he said. 'There are plays and concerts staged here throughout the summer.'

Her face lit up. 'Really? I would love to attend one. I wouldn't care what it was, just to be here would be the most amazing experience. Please, Alex, can you help me book a performance before I go home?'

Alex paused for a moment too long and the silence fell awkwardly between them. He knew she would have to go back to Sydney for the birth of her baby, but didn't want to think about the gap her loss would leave in his life. Almost as if he didn't acknowledge it, it wouldn't happen. 'Of course,' he said eventually, forcing himself not to sound glum.

As they continued the climb, glimpses of the immense marble columns of the Parthenon above them beckoned. 'There it is!' Dell paused, gawking above her, and tripped over the uneven paving on the pathway. 'I wondered if I would ever get to see it.'

'Careful,' Alex said as he took her elbow to steady her. He intended to keep a grip on her but she flushed and he loosened his hold.

'I'm okay,' she said.

'A woman in your condition isn't supposed to fall,' he said.

'Condition?' she said with a quirk of her auburn brows. 'You make it sound like something medical. Being pregnant is something natural for a woman. Something wonderful.'

'But you've been so ill,' he said, remembering the day he'd seen her in Nidri, how her haggard appearance had shocked him.

'That's just the hormones, the doctor told me. All part of the process of pregnancy. Some women suffer more than others. I don't need to be wrapped in cotton wool.' She looked up at him with a sweet curving of her lips. 'Although

I do appreciate your concern. It's very chival-rous of you.'

'So long as you're okay.' Chivalrous? Alex didn't think he'd ever been called that before. Selfish. Inconsiderate. Arrogant. That was what he'd been used to in his past. He tried on the feel of *chivalrous* and liked it, though he really was only doing what came naturally when he was around Dell.

'I'm actually more than okay.' She breathed deeply as she looked around her, at the steep hill wooded in parts with cypress and olive. If you looked closely there were spring flowers in the undergrowth and Alex pointed them out to her. She took a few snaps with her smartphone.

'Thank you,' she said. 'I don't know anything about the plants here. And you never know what can make an interesting blog post.'

'The ten minutes you spent reading the poster on "Vegetation and Flora of the Acropolis" must surely have helped,' he said with a smile.

'Did I spend that long?' she said. 'I'm sorry. I'm fascinated with everything about this place.'

'I like that,' he said. He was learning that Dell was never satisfied with skimming the surface, she had to dig deep, to learn. It was one of the reasons she made such a good employee and why he valued her more each day.

'Being on this ancient ground, I can't help thinking of all the people who have been here before us, all the people who are to come,' she said. 'I'm bearing a new life. It makes me feel connected, part of something much greater.'

A new life? Alex had not thought of her pregnancy in that way, perhaps he hadn't wanted to. He had seen it as an inconvenience, limiting the months she could work for him, blocking the possibility of pursuing his attraction to her. Not as the growth of a new little person who would make Dell a mother. She would be a good mother, he thought. But what about the father? What role would he play in her life? He felt a stab of discomfort at the thought of her ex. He refused to consider it could be jealousy.

Dell placed her hand on her stomach. She was wearing a wearing a white dress of soft cotton that flowed around her body. He realised with a shock that she was probably wearing it because it was looser than what she usually wore. It tied under her breasts with a blue woven tie. He noticed a new curve to her belly. Were her breasts bigger too? A quick glance said they were. Her new curves made her even lovelier.

She must have noticed the direction of his gaze. She smiled. 'I've started to show. Now I'm letting myself really believe I'm having a baby. Did you notice me tugging at my skirt during the meetings today? I tried not to make it obvious, but it's getting very tight.'

'You're happy about that?' he said.

'Really happy,' she said without hesitation. Alex could see from the glow of her face and the joy in her eyes that she meant it. 'The timing isn't the most convenient, I acknowledge that. But I've wanted a baby for so long and this is probably my only chance.'

'What will you do when you go back to Sydney?' he asked.

A little of the glow faded. 'I'll have to fling myself on the mercy of my parents.'

He frowned. 'Wouldn't they be delighted they were going to be grandparents? My sisters both have children. Nothing makes my parents happier than their grandbabies.'

He wondered if they'd given up hope for any grandchildren from him. He had been so busy turning partying into a multimillion-dollar business he hadn't actually thought much about children. He'd always wanted to have kids but it had been filed in the 'one day' category—even with Mia, who had also thought of babies as something for the future.

'From what I've heard about your family, that doesn't surprise me,' she said. 'My parents are very different. They're not really family orientated. We're not close. They'll be shocked at what I've done. I'm just hoping they won't disapprove so much they won't help me.'

'Can't you live on your own? Don't you have your own apartment in Sydney?'

She shook her head. 'I came off the worst in

the spoils of divorce. He got the apartment, I got the debts.' Her attempt to sound flippant failed miserably.

'Can you expect support from your ex?'

'No way. I…er…I'm not sure I'll even tell him. He's married again, has a new life. We're not in touch.'

He frowned. 'Doesn't he have a right to know he's going to be a father?'

'I'm not sure that he does,' she said, tight-lipped. Alex could read the *don't go there* signals flashing from her eyes. But the little she gave away made him believe she had reason to be wary of the ex. The guy sounded like a jerk.

'So you'll be going back to Sydney to nothing?'

'That's not quite true. My parents have a large house. Even if simply out of duty I'm sure they'll find room for me and the baby until I get on my feet again. Though to tell you the truth, I'm not looking forward to telling them my news.'

'Your parents don't know you're pregnant?'

'No one does but you, and my doctor in Nidri,

of course.' She looked up at him, her eyes huge. 'I've been disappointed so many times. I'm waiting until I'm further down the track before I tell anyone. Just in case.'

Pain shadowed her eyes and he realised how desperately she wanted this pregnancy, how vulnerable it made her and how alone she seemed in the world. He felt angry her parents sounded so distant, that they wouldn't want to help her at such a time. As for the ex, Alex's fists clenched beside him. Again that fierce desire to protect her swept over him. He couldn't bear to think of her struggling on her own. Life could be tough for a lone parent. He knew that from the juggling some of his single-mother staff had had to do to keep an income coming in. How would Dell manage?

This was not his baby. Not his business. But *she* was his business. He had brought her to Greece and she had proved herself tuned to the same wavelength as he was when it came to the business. The plans for the hotel would not be moving along so quickly or so efficiently without her help. He'd have to find a way to give her a substantial bonus before she left his employment. Otherwise, he didn't know how he could help her.

But there was one way he could help her now. He took her hand in his. 'Come on, let's get up to the top. But I'm going to make sure you don't stumble again. You're stuck with my chivalry.'

This time she smiled and didn't pull away. He folded her much smaller hand in his; the answering pressure made him feel inordinately pleased. When they reached a smoother part of the path he didn't let go of her hand.

With each step forward up the hill Dell silently chanted a *what if?* inside her head. What if Alex was holding her hand because he wanted to, not just out of consideration of her pregnant condition? What if they were a genuine couple, linking hands as they always did when they walked together out on a date? What if she were pregnant to a man like him—she couldn't go so far as to fantasise she was actually pregnant to *him*. Then there was the biggest *what if* of them all, one she scarcely dared breathe for fear of jinxing herself: what if she weren't pregnant and she were free to explore her attraction to Alex, to flirt a little, let him know how she felt, act upon it? *What if he felt the same?*

He kept hold of her hand as they reached the top and at last the Parthenon towered above her. The ground was rough, broken stone and marble caused by ongoing repairs and the tramping of thousands—possibly millions—of feet across the ancient land over the centuries. She had to be careful she didn't go over on her ankle.

'Wow, just wow,' she breathed as she gazed up the iconic structure, which no photo or painting could do justice. Built around 432 BC as a temple to worship the Goddess Athena, it had been scarred by attacks and battle over the centuries. Yet its remaining pillars and sculptures still stood overlooking Athens, an imposing edifice to an ancient civilisation.

'You're so lucky to have this as your heritage,' she said with awe.

'It's the world's heritage,' he said, his voice edged with pride.

Dell had long realised how important his Greekness was to Alex. Would he ever go back to Australia? Would she ever see him again after she went back?

For a long time she stood gazing in wonder at the magnificence of the ancient building with its massive columns and pediments achingly beautiful against a clear blue sky. It made it poignant that she was sharing it with Alex—boss, friend, man she longed to be so more than that if things were different.

She looked up at him, so tall and broad-shouldered, handsome in light linen trousers and white shirt, his dark hair longer now than when she'd first seen him at Bay Breeze, curling around his temples. Her heart seemed to flip over. 'Thank you, Alex. I'll never forget this moment, here with you in the land of your ancestors.'

He looked back down at her for a long moment. She could tell by the deepened intensity of his dark eyes that he was going to kiss her and a tremor of anticipation rippled through her. At that moment, it was what she wanted more than anything in the world. She swayed towards him, not breaking the connection of their eyes, her lips parting in expectation of his mouth on hers. And then he was kissing her.

His mouth was firm and warm, a gentle respectful touch asking a question that she answered by tilting her head to better kiss him back. *Bliss.* This was one small dream that was coming true. Dell realised she had closed her eyes and she opened them again, not wanting to miss anything of this—touch, taste, his scent, the sight of his face. She found his eyes intent on hers and she smiled. He smiled back and then kissed her again. They exchanged a series of short, sweet kisses that escalated with a subtle sensuality that left her breathless.

She was dimly aware that they were still standing with the Parthenon behind them, in one of the most public arenas in Athens. But when he pulled her closer into a longer, more intense embrace she forgot where she was. All she was aware of was Alex—the feel of his arms holding her close, her arms twined around his neck, his mouth, his tongue, the fierce strength of his body. Every kiss she'd ever had faded into insignificance. *This.* Alex.

'Bravo!' Good-natured catcalls and cheering broke into the bliss and she realised they had an audience. She doubted anyone knew who Alex was, but there were a lot of smartphones around. Everyone was a potential *paparazzo* these days.

She broke away from the kiss although she couldn't keep the smile from her voice. 'That was probably not a good idea,' she murmured. On one level she meant kissing in public. On another, she meant shifting their relationship to something more personal wasn't either. If, indeed, that was what this had signalled.

'Yes, it wasn't,' he said with rather too much vehemence. The shutters came down over his eyes again, leaving them black and unreadable. He took an abrupt step back and tripped on the uneven ground. Dell had to catch his arm and hold him steady. But she didn't care about his less than romantic reaction. This day could end right now and she would be happy. Alex had kissed her and she would treasure the moment for ever. No matter what might or might not follow.

'Thank you,' he said. Then, his voice hoarse, 'Thank you for rescuing me.'

'All I did was help you keep your balance,' she said.

'You've done that all right,' he said and she realised they were speaking at a deeper level. 'But you've done so much more.' He reached down to trace a line from her cheekbone to the edge of her mouth. His touch sent a shiver of pleasure through her. 'I didn't think I could be attracted to another woman after…after Mia. But you've proved me wrong.'

'Was…was kissing me some kind of experiment?' She tried to mask the hurt in her voice with a light-hearted tone.

His face darkened. 'No. How could you think that? You looked so lovely, so warm and vibrant with laughter in your eyes, I simply couldn't resist you.'

Warmth flooded through her heart, only to chill at his next words. 'Even though I know I should not have done so. Dell, I—'

Her spirits plummeted to somewhere around her shoes. She put a hand up to halt him. 'Please, we still have an audience.'

He glared at the people watching them and they hastily dispersed.

Dell looked around her. 'It's getting hot. Can we find somewhere with some shade?'

Shade was in short supply on the Acropolis. But they managed to find a patch as they headed across to the Temple of Diana. Dell forced a laugh as they seated themselves on one of the large chunks of marble lying around the site. 'Is this marble a part of the Parthenon and an archaeological treasure, or destined to be used in the restoration? I can't believe there's so much marble scattered around the place.'

'The latter I suspect,' Alex said, obviously not interested in talking about marble, perhaps aware she was using it as a stalling tactic. He spoke bluntly. 'Dell, I meant what I said before. I find you very attractive in every way but you're pregnant to another man and that puts you out of bounds.'

'I...I see,' she said, thinking back to her list of *what ifs*. She took a deep steadying breath against a twisting stab of disappointment. 'I appreciate your honesty, understand where you're coming from. A lot of men would probably feel the same way, I imagine. That doesn't stop me from being delighted I'm pregnant.' Her eyes dropped, so did her voice. 'What it does make me feel is regret...regret that maybe we didn't meet at a different time or place.' She looked up at him again. 'For the record, I find you very attractive. I...I like you too, which is a surprise as I used to loathe you.'

His laugh was broken and rough. 'I can't imagine how I could ever have considered you an enemy,' he said.

He went to kiss her again but Dell put her finger across his lips to stop him. 'No. That last kiss—that *first* kiss was perfect. Let's not override it with a kiss of regret and…what might have been.'

She took his hand in hers. 'But please, hold my hand for the rest of the day, because I couldn't bear it if you didn't.'

'As you wish, although I would kiss you with no regret.' He folded her hand into his much bigger one.

She took a deep breath to keep her voice steady. 'When we get back to Kosmimo, I suggest we pretend this never happened. That we agree you're my boss and I'm your assistant. We go back to the status quo, as it can never be anything more than that between us. I…I couldn't bear working with you, sharing the pavilion with you, if it was any other way.' If ever there was a time for her fluffy-chick face, this was it.

But when in defiance of her feeble ban he lifted her hand to his lips and pressed a kiss into the sensitive centre of her palm, she did not object. She could not let a betraying quiver in her voice let him guess she was crying deep down inside her heart.

CHAPTER TWELVE

TRUE TO HER WORD, Dell didn't refer again to their trip to the Acropolis. Alex wasn't sure if he was surprised or relieved at the way she had totally wiped from their agenda their kiss in front of the columns of the Parthenon.

During the week they'd been back, she deftly changed the subject if anything regarding that day threatened to sneak into the conversation. He had even looked on her *Dell Dishes* blog to see what she had posted about her trip to Athens.

She wrote about her climb of the Acropolis and shared food images from the Athens restaurants where they had eaten together. But without a mention of him. *'My companion,'* she referred to when describing her climb. Her neuter-general companion was what he had been relegated to. Common sense told him that was perfectly appropriate. He should appreciate her discretion. It was insane to feel excluded. Not when he was the one who had called the shots.

At the office she was bright, efficient and as totally professional as she should be. As if she had never murmured her pleasure at his kiss with a sweet little hitch to her voice.

It was he who felt unsatisfied. Grumpy. Frustrated. Because just that taste of her lips had awakened a hunger for her. A need. If he could take her to bed and make love to her before she showed any further signs of pregnancy, pretend she wasn't expecting another man's baby, he would. Only he knew it would be the wrong thing to do. For him, for *her*. Because he liked her enough not to want to hurt her. And sex without commitment, whether she was pregnant or not, was not something that Dell would welcome. He sensed that, *knew* that.

Yet how ironic that the further she got into her pregnancy, the more she bloomed and the more beautiful she appeared. He had heard the word *blooming* used to describe expectant women but had never had an idea what it meant. She was still barely showing but she was curvier in the right places, her hair appeared thicker and glossier, her skin glowed and her eyes seemed a brighter shade of green.

On occasion her complexion was greener too. But her morning sickness seemed to be easing. Soon she might be able to handle the daily crossing between Nidri and Kosmima and go back to stay in Aunt Penelope's villa. But she didn't mention it and neither did he.

Alex liked having her in the pavilion, even though she studiously avoided any potential moments of intimacy. Even though it was frustrating knowing she was in the bedroom next to him—each of them all alone in those super-sized beds. Because her presence—her light, quick footsteps on the marble floor, snatches of her voice as she hummed a Greek song his aunt had taught her as she moved around the kitchen— was comforting.

He realised for the first time in a long time he didn't feel lonely. The nightmares about Mia in the clutches of the gunman had abated. Thanks to Dell. He dreaded how empty the rooms would seem when she went back to Australia to have her baby.

He felt like humming himself—although he never did anything so unmanly—as he checked the latest reports from the architects and designers. They were well on track; in fact some of the rooms in the hotel were already just about ready for occupancy. It was pleasing.

Dell had still been in the pavilion earlier this morning as he had headed over to the main building and their shared office. He hadn't enquired about her estimated time to start work. It was likely she wasn't well. Not that she'd let her morning sickness interfere in any way with her work. That added another notch to his admiration of her; he knew how difficult it must be.

This morning he was impatient for her to get to her desk. He wanted to share his exultation that things were going so well. Because she had contributed to it with her keen eye and smart observations. Not to mention her meticulous record-keeping. Another thing that pleased him was her handling of publicity. Her careful drip-feeding of snippets about the launch, her forward-planning of interviews and media site visits were beginning to create the low-level buzz he had hoped for. He had every reason to pay her that bonus—sooner rather than later perhaps.

He looked up from his desk as he heard her footsteps approach, dragging rather than tip-tapping on the marble. Alarmed, he leapt to his feet. Was she ill again?

But when she entered the room Dell looked more distressed than sick. Her face was flushed, high on her cheekbones, her eyes glittered, and her hands were balled into fists. 'Sorry I'm late,' she said, tight-lipped.

'Dell, what's going on?'

'Nothing,' she said.

'That's obviously not true.'

She gave a great sigh that wrenched at him.

'I don't want to bring my personal problems to work.'

'Where else can you take them right now?'

That forced a glimmer of a smile from her. 'Are you sure you want to hear this?'

If it had been anyone other than Dell, he would have beat a hasty retreat. Girl problems were something to be avoided. But she really didn't have anyone else with whom to share her obvious angst. 'Fire away,' he said.

She stood by her desk, feet braced as if steeling herself. 'I just had a horrible, abusive call from my ex-husband, Neil. He's found out that I'm pregnant.'

'How? You said no one else knows but me and your doctor.'

Alex swore he could hear her teeth grinding. 'The stupidest of mix-ups. The fertility clinic sent a letter to me at his address—which was my old address. Seemed they'd sent it to me at my rented apartment and it had been returned, even though I paid for a redirection order on my mail. So they sent it to the previous address they had for me. Needless to say I'm furious at them. And at the darn post office.'

'Your ex opened a letter that was addressed to you?'

'That would be typical—he always thought my business was his business. I…I used to think his controlling ways were because he cared. Boy, did I get to know better towards the end.'

Alex hated to see the bitter twist of her mouth. The more he heard about her ex, the less he liked him. 'You said he was abusive?'

'Furious. Shouting. Making threats. Said he refused to have anything to do with the baby. That…that the embryo should have been destroyed. That I…that I had no right to take it. That…I was utterly selfish to have done what I did. That I…I wasn't thinking of anyone else but myself.'

'I'm so sorry, Dell. If there's anything I can do—'

'Thank you but, despite how vile he's being, he did have some right to be angry. I don't regret undertaking the procedure but I knew it probably wasn't the right thing to do. We weren't married any more. Circumstances were entirely different.'

Alex wanted to draw her into a hug but he knew it would not be welcome. In spite of all his business expertise he honestly didn't know how he could help her make the best of the complex and unusual situation she found herself in. But his thoughts were racing. He knew a lot of people in Sydney. People who could track down this guy. Keep an eye on Dell's ex. Report back to Alex so he could make sure Dell wasn't under any threat. He worried about her going back to Sydney on her own.

'What else did he have to say?'

'Again and again that he would deny paternity. That being a sperm donor didn't make him a father.'

'Good point. And why would you want him as the father?'

She made a gesture of despair with her hands. 'I guess he has good genes. He's handsome.

Intelligent. Good at sport. I used to think he was kind.'

'What does the guy do for a living?'

'He's a civil engineer.'

Alex groaned.

'What was that for?' Dell asked.

'You should have added boring to his list of genetic attributes.'

That elicited a watery smile from Dell. 'I guess I should. He always was a tad on the dull side. But I traded that for security. How did I put up with it for so long?'

'Because you really wanted a kid and you thought he'd be a safe bet?'

'Something like that, I guess,' she said. 'There I was married and living in the suburbs at age twenty-two while you were building up your fortune.'

'Partying was a far less boring profession,' he said. 'But back then you wouldn't have looked at me, would you?'

'Probably not. I was far too prim.'

'Were you really? I find that very difficult

to believe. I suspect you're a very passionate woman. When I kissed you I—'

'That's a no-go zone, Alex,' she warned. 'Can we change the subject?'

'Back to your boring, bad-tempered husband?'

That brought another smile. 'If you put it that way. Actually, I think I'll think of him that way from now on—Neil the BBTH.'

'The Boring Bad-Tempered *Ex*-Husband, you mean,' he said.

She giggled. 'Okay, the BBT Ex-H.' He was glad he could make her laugh. The phone call must have been traumatic.

'It's a mouthful. Why not settle on BX, *boring ex*, for short?' he said. He could think of much worse things he could call her odious former husband. 'Boring is worse than bad-tempered. We all have our bad-tempered moments.'

'BX he shall be from now on.' She sobered. 'Deep down I guess I hoped he might want to have some kind of contact—for the baby's sake, not mine. Back then he wanted a child as much as I did. But perhaps he didn't. Perhaps he's right. Am I being selfish in having this child on my own? Maybe it's always been about my need to have a baby.'

'Isn't that how most people decide to have children? Because they want them?' he asked. 'Not that I know a lot about it.'

'Perhaps. But that's all beside the point, isn't it? I'm going to love this baby enough for two parents. There are worse ways to come into the world than being utterly loved, aren't there?' She sounded in need of reassurance.

'Indeed,' he said. 'Your baby will be lucky to have a mother like you.'

But a child needed a father. Alex had had his differences with his father, but he'd always been there loving and supporting him. Dell's child would grow up without that constant male presence. Of course, she might marry again, meet someone like Jesse Morgan who would be a father to her child. He pulled the 'off' switch on that train of thought. He couldn't bear to think of Dell with another man. He'd been called selfish too.

'One last thing the BX told me was that his new wife was pregnant. Therefore all the problems we had were my fault.' Her voice broke. 'There was nothing wrong with him—no, siree—it was *me* who was the failure. Me who put him through all that. And if I insisted on going ahead with this pregnancy I'd better get myself checked out to see if I was actually capable of carrying a child.' Her last words came out so choked he could hardly hear them.

Alex could feel a bad-tempered moment of mammoth proportions threatening to erupt. Was there a hitman among all those contacts in Sydney? He ran through all the swear words he knew in both English and Greek. None was strong enough to express his contempt for Dell's ex-husband.

He gritted his teeth. 'Lucky he's not here because if he was I'd—'

'Whatever you'd do I'd do worse.'

'Dell, you're better off without that…that jerk. So is your child.'

'You're absolutely right. In some ways the encounter with him is a relief. I don't have to worry about the BX ever again.' Dell spat out the initials so they came out sounding like the worst kind of swear words. She took a deep, heaving breath. 'I was so worried about him, now I won't have to worry. If he denies paternity, that's good too. It might make it easier for me to get help if that's the case.'

'What do you mean?'

'Back home in Sydney, if I have to apply for a supporting mothers' benefit, I will have to name the father and try to get support from him—something I never intended to do, by the way. If I put "father unknown" it might not make me look very good but I could get help for a while if needed.'

Anguish that this spirited, warm, intelligent woman should be in that position tore through him. 'Dell, don't go back to Sydney. Have the baby here. You're entitled to maternity leave. Your job would still be waiting for you. You wouldn't have to beg for help from your parents or the government or anyone else.'

Tears glistened in her green eyes and she scrubbed them away with her finger. It left a smear of black make-up that made her look more woebegone. 'Thank you, Alex. That's incredibly kind of you. I love it here but…but I don't want to give birth to my baby surrounded by strangers. I have to go home, no matter what I might face.'

Alex stared at her for a long moment. *A stranger.* That was all he was to her. *That was all he'd let himself be.* The realisation felt like another giant kick to his gut.

He had to pull himself together, not let her know how her words had affected him. 'The offer is still there,' he said.

'Thank you,' she said again. 'I truly appreciate it.' She squared her shoulders. 'But we have work to do.' She didn't seem to realise she was wringing her hands together. 'Now that we've got personal, it might be time for me to ask you about Mia. I have to know how to spin your story before the media goes off on their own wild tangents. I'm going to fix my face. When I get back I need to talk to you.'

Mia. When would he ever be able to talk about his guilt over what had happened? But if there was anyone he could open up to, it would be Dell.

CHAPTER THIRTEEN

DELL HAD BEEN trying to bring up the story of Alex's late fiancée for some time but she'd never quite found the courage to do so. The stricken look on his face told her no time would be the right time.

'I…I'm sorry if I sounded blunt,' she said. 'But you know the launch of the resort will mean you coming back into the spotlight. As soon as that happens all the stories of the siege and…and Mia's death will be resuscitated. The personal story will always override the business one. I don't need to remind you that the anniversary of the siege is coming up. Let's give the media a story before they go burrowing for one.'

Alex slid both hands through his hair to cradle his head with such an abject look it tore at her heart. 'I knew this was coming,' he said. 'I suppose I can't put it off for longer?'

Dell shook her head. She felt mean forcing him to talk. But this was about helping launch his new venture. 'If we could give an exclusive interview to, say, one of the weekend newspaper magazines we might be able to control it to some degree.'

Alex looked barely capable of standing. 'Why don't we sit over on the chairs so I can take notes?' she suggested tactfully.

'Sure,' he said.

Once they were seated—him opposite her, so close she had to slant her legs to avoid their knees touching—she decided to conduct this as if it were an interview.

'Alex, I know how difficult this is for you. Well, I don't really have any idea but I'm trying to imagine the unimaginable. I'm aware that Mia was the love of your life and what a tremendous blow it must have been to have lost her under such shocking and public circumstances. After she…she died you disappeared from Sydney.

What people will want to know is where you went, why you did so, and how it led to the development of Pevezzo Athina. Try to answer me so we can work out what we tell the media.'

He was silent for a long time. Dell became very aware she might be overstepping the mark. But this was her job, why he had brought her to Greece. She wasn't interviewing Alex her boss, her friend, the man she was in serious danger of falling in love with. This was Alexios Mikhalis, multimillionaire tycoon, ruthless businessman, man who'd led a charmed life until that terrible moment a maniac had walked into his restaurant brandishing a gun and had grabbed Alex's beautiful fiancée as hostage.

The silence was getting uncomfortable before he finally spoke, his words slow and measured. 'As far as the media is concerned, I was so devastated by the tragic loss of my fiancée I decided to get as far away from Sydney as possible. It made sense that I went to Greece, to the place my grandfather came from, where I still had extended family and could remain anonymous. I stayed with my relatives, worked with them on their fishing boats and in their olive groves, even waited tables in the family *taverna*.'

'Getting your hands dirty? Grounding yourself?'

'That's a good way to put it,' he said. 'You could say I found peace in the glorious surroundings and wanted to share it with others. I came up with the concept of a holistic resort where our guests could also find peace.'

Dell scribbled on her notepad, not wanting to meet his eyes, too scared of what she might see there. 'Have you found peace, Alex?'

'I'm still seeking it. I think you know that.'

She looked up. 'Can I say guests can come to heal?' she asked tentatively. 'Like you healed?'

'You can say that,' he said.

Could the scars he bore ever really heal? For the press release she had to take his words at surface value.

'And you bought a private island? The media will be very interested in that.'

'That is a matter of public record, so yes, I

should certainly talk about Kosmimo. Not, however, about the most recent owner.'

'What about the island's link to your family?'

'Many years ago, Kosmimo was owned by my ancestors. Circumstances conspired to allow me to buy it back. I will never let the island get out of my family's hands again.'

Dell turned a new page of her notebook. 'Sounds like the perfect sound bite. That will make an excellent story. Especially back in Sydney with the city's obsession with real estate.'

He cracked a half-smile at that. She braced herself for the next question, knowing it would vanquish his smile. 'Alex, I have to ask about your private life.'

As predicted, his smile tightened into a grim line. 'I have no private life,' he said. 'The media will find nothing titillating about me and other women.'

Unless someone recognised him kissing his assistant on the Acropolis, Dell thought.

'Because you could never find a woman to live up to Mia?'

'You can tell that to the media,' he said. 'But the truth is quite different.' He leaned forward with his hands on his knees so his face was only inches from her. She breathed in the already familiar scent of him. The scent that made her feel giddy with the hopelessness of her crush on him, made even deeper by those kisses on the Acropolis. Kisses she revisited every night in her dreams.

'The truth is only for your ears,' he continued. 'I meant what I said on the Acropolis that day.'

She held her breath not daring to say anything, realising how important this was to him. And perhaps significant to her.

'The truth is I feel so damn guilty I sent Mia to her death that I will never be able to commit to another woman.' His eyes were shadowed with immeasurable sorrow.

Dell gasped. 'But you didn't send her to her death. How could you possibly believe that? The gunman chose your restaurant at random. It was sheer bad luck Mia was there at the time.

It could have been any of your staff. It could have been *you*.'

His face darkened in a grimace, his voice was grave and low. 'You don't know how many times I wished it had been me…'

Dell swallowed hard. She didn't know that she was capable of replying the right way to such a statement. But out of compassion—and her regard for him—she would try. 'Alex, you can't mean that. You cannot punish yourself for something that was completely out of your hands.'

He spoke through gritted teeth. 'It was my fault Mia was there that day. It should have been her day off.'

Dell frowned. 'I don't get it.'

'Here's something you wouldn't have read in the press. I insisted she go in to work when the head chef was injured in an accident. Mia and I argued about that. One argument led to another. Until it ended up where it always ended up. My tardiness in setting a date for the wedding. We hadn't resolved it when she stormed out. Mia went to her death worrying that I didn't really love her. That's what I can't live with.'

Dell realised she had been holding her breath. She let it out in a long sigh. 'Oh, Alex. I'm so sorry.' She reached out and laid her hand on top of his. 'But you were engaged to be married. She would have known you loved her.'

He choked out the words. 'Or suspected that I didn't love her enough.'

'I can't believe that's true.'

He got up from the chair. Started to pace the room. Dell got up too, stood anchored by the edge of her desk. She had long stopped taking notes. These revelations were strictly off the record.

'You have to understand the place I was in at the time I met Mia. Settling down with one woman hadn't been on the agenda. I was growing the business at a relentless pace. One new venture after the other.'

'To prove you could do it, to prove to your family that you'd made the right choices for yourself.'

He stopped his pacing. 'That's perceptive of you. I'd never thought of it that way, but you're right.'

'It left no time for dating?' She knew about the string of glamorous blonde women he had been seen with on any social occasion where a photographer had been present.

'I made it very clear to the women I dated that I was not interested in commitment. I didn't have the time, or the inclination.'

'Then you met Mia.' Their love story had been rehashed over and over again in the media.

'Mia...she made me change my mind.'

'She was beautiful.' It hurt Dell to talk about the woman who had won his heart and met such a tragic end. But she wanted to understand him. And not just because she needed to for her job. That was the craziness of a crush on a man who wanted nothing to do with you. You wanted to find out everything you could about him. Because that was all you would ever have.

'Mia was beautiful, fun, a super-talented chef and liked to party hard and work hard like I did.

I was smitten. I still didn't feel ready to settle down. But if I wanted Mia in my life I had to make a commitment or lose her. Those were her terms.'

'Quite rightly too,' Dell murmured in sudden solidarity with his late fiancée.

He paused. 'She would have liked you.'

'I think I might have liked her.' Would she have been jealous of Mia? It was a pointless question. Back then she'd been too busy with her marriage and her desire to start a family to even think about another man. No matter how attractive. No matter how unattainable.

'I can tell myself over and over that it was fate she was in the restaurant at the wrong time. But fate had nothing to do with me beginning to question if Mia was the right person to be my lifetime partner. And not being honest enough to tell her.'

'So that's where the guilt comes from,' Dell said slowly. 'But if you don't forgive yourself you'll go crazy. Mia loved you. She wouldn't have wanted you to live your life alone. It's been nearly three years, Alex. Wouldn't she have wanted you to move on?'

'Meeting you showed me I could be attracted to another woman, Dell. I thought that would never happen. You don't want to talk about that day in Athens. But I meant what I said. That doesn't mean I intend to commit to another woman ever again.'

'It's as well I'm out of bounds because of my pregnancy, then,' she said, trying to sound as uninterested as if she were discussing someone else.

For her own self-protection she had to do that. Did he realise how hurtful he sounded? Or was he still so caught up in his grief and guilt he didn't realise that the best thing that could happen to him was to let himself love again? If not with her then with someone else. And when that happened, she wanted to be far, far away.

CHAPTER FOURTEEN

THREE PEOPLE INVITED Dell to the party to celebrate Alex's Aunt Penelope's seventy-fifth birthday on the coming Saturday. Aunt Penelope herself. Alex's cousin Cristos. And then Alex.

Dell had told the first two she would have to check with Alex before she could accept. She hadn't missed their exchange of sly smiles at her words. She had protested that Alex was her boss and she was accountable to him. Aunt Penelope had replied, with a knowing nod, that in Greece the man was always the boss. Dell had decided not to argue with the older woman on that one.

When Alex invited her to the party she told him about the other two. His eyes narrowed at the mention of the invitation from Cristos. Surely he couldn't be jealous of his handsome cousin? She quite liked the little flicker of satisfaction she got from that. Cristos was, in fact, extraordinarily good-looking. But the only man Dell had eyes for was Alex. Much good that it did her.

'The party will be at the original Taverna Athina on Prasinos,' he said. 'Of course you will come. I promised to take you there one day, if you recall.'

'I'm honoured to be invited,' she said. 'But do you think it's wise, considering the ongoing speculation about us as…well, as a couple?' She laid her hand on her gently rounded belly. 'It's getting harder to conceal my pregnancy.'

'Your pregnancy is your business,' he said. *And nothing to do with me.* Dell sensed his unspoken words. 'You don't owe an explanation to anyone in my family. When it becomes obvious you're expecting you can tell them whatever version of the story behind it you choose.'

'In that case, I happily accept the invitation. All three invitations.'

'But you'll be coming to the party with me,' said Alex.

An imp of mischief prompted Dell's retort. 'But Cristos said he'd take me in his boat.'

Alex glowered down at her. 'You will *not* go in my cousin's boat. You will go in my boat. It's much more comfortable and better for a woman in your—'

'Condition, I know,' she said. 'Of course your boat is far superior to Cristos's boat. Your boat is superior to any other man's boat I know. Not that I know another person who owns a super duper speedboat like yours.' What was lacking in his four-by-four Alex kept on Nidri, and the equally battered van he kept on Kosmimo, was more than made up for in his luxurious streamlined boat.

'You'd better believe it,' he said with a reluctant grin. 'Cristos can transport his grandparents Aunt Penelope and Uncle Stavros to the party.'

'Befitting as she is the guest of honour,' Dell said.

'The party starts in the afternoon and might go on quite late,' he said. 'The *taverna* also has rooms to rent. I will book one for you so you can stay overnight. If you get tired you can slip away any time.'

'And you?' she said.

'I'll bunk down at my uncle's house. It's where I stayed when I first arrived from Australia. It's on the same street so I won't be far should you need me.'

'I'll be okay,' she said, hoping that was the case. Anyone she had met from his family had been friendly and hospitable, while being subtly—or not so subtly, depending on gender—interested in her relationship with Alex. 'I'm looking forward to it.'

Taverna Athina was set right on the beach at the southernmost corner of a delightfully curving bay. The water rippled from sapphire, to the palest aquamarine, to crystal clear lapping up on a beach comprising tiny pale pebbles.

The open-air dining area of the *taverna*—entirely reserved today for the family party—sat right over the water on a dock. A banner was strung from post to post with a message in the

Greek alphabet that Dell assumed meant Happy Birthday but Alex explained read *hronia polla*, and was a wish for many more happy years of life.

The *taverna* was painted white with accents of bright blue and tubs of Greek basil at its corners. The effect was friendly and welcoming. Behind the *taverna* was a traditional Greek building with a terracotta-tiled roof. Its idyllic position with the tree-studded hill as background and the water in front made it look as if the restaurant could sail off at any moment.

'That's where you'll be staying,' said Alex, indicating the older building as he helped her off his boat, moored nearby. 'It's humble but comfortable.'

'The *taverna* is charming, Alex,' she said. 'No wonder you were so attached to Athina in Sydney if this was its parentage.'

Greek music, typical of the Ionian Islands, was echoing out onto the beach. 'It's what Tia Penelope likes,' Alex explained.

'I like it too,' said Dell.

She held back as she and Alex got near to the *taverna* entrance, suddenly aware of her ambivalent status as employee and yet friend enough to be invited to a family party. And then there was the persistent speculation about her and Alex as an item.

She need not have worried. As soon as she got inside she was swept up by Aunt Penelope and introduced to the family members she hadn't previously met at either the villa or on Kosmimo. She told herself she was imagining it that the first thing the women did was glance down at her stomach.

As she was being carried away Dell turned to see Alex in animated conversation with a tall older man with steel-grey hair and glasses and an elegantly dressed woman of about the same age who had her arm looped through Alex's as though she could never let him go. Dell had no idea who they were. But even from a distance, she could see Alex bore a distinct resemblance to the man. Perhaps they had come from Athens for the party.

* * *

'What are you doing here?' Alex asked his parents, still reeling from his shock at seeing them at the *taverna*. 'I had no idea you were coming.'

'A surprise for Penelope for her birthday,' his father said. 'She says she's getting too old to fly all the way to Australia so we decided to come to her.' His father's voice was husky as if he had a heavy cold. He was getting older now, surely he shouldn't have flown with a cold.

'We wanted to see you, too, catch up with how you're doing,' said his mother.

That made sense. But Alex detected an unfamiliar restraint to the tone of both his parents' voices and wondered. 'Why didn't you tell me?' he said.

'We thought it could be a surprise for you too,' said his mother, unconvincingly to Alex's ears.

'It's certainly that,' said Alex. 'Where are you staying?'

'Here at the *taverna*,' his father replied. 'Where we always stay when we visit the family.'

Alex's father was a highly regarded orthopaedic surgeon back in Sydney, his mother a sports physiotherapist of some renown. They could afford to stay in the best of hotels. Fact was, on Prasinos the two-star Athina was the best hotel. There were luxury villas and houses to be rented but the family would take great offence if his parents stayed anywhere but the family hotel.

'We saw you come in with that lovely red-haired girl Penelope has been telling us about.'

'You mean my assistant, Dell Hudson?' Alex asked, forcing his voice to stay steady.

'Is that all she is?' said his mother, sounding disappointed. 'Penelope led me to believe there was something more between you. You know how much we want you to be happy after Mia and—'

'Dell is a very capable employee, that's all,' Alex said through gritted teeth.

Was his aunt just speculating or did she at some level recognise how attracted he was to Dell? Whatever, he wished she would stop the gossiping. The sideways glances and speculation from the rest of the family were beginning to get uncomfortable. There were handwritten name-cards at each table place. Someone had thought it funny to strike out *Dell Hudson* to be replaced by *Dell Mikhalis*. He had grabbed it and crumpled it into his pocket before Dell could have a chance to see it.

His father frowned. 'Wasn't Adele Hudson the woman who gave Athina that bad review? When you sued the newspaper and lost all that money.'

'Yes,' he said.

'So why are you employing her?' said his mother. 'Is this a case of keeping your friends close and your enemies closer?'

Why was this conversation centring on Dell? 'She's not an enemy. In fact she was right about the falling standards at the restaurant. I employed her because she's really smart and switched on. She's proved to be immensely valuable to me on my new venture.'

'Oh,' said his mother again. Alex gritted his teeth even harder.

He looked over to see Dell helping out by carrying a tray of *meze*, an assortment of Greek appetisers, to the buffet table. Dell was laughing at something Aunt Penelope was saying. Among his mostly dark-haired family she stood out with her bright hair and her strapless dress in multiple shades of blue that reflected the colours of the Ionian Sea. She had never looked lovelier. Alex could see exactly why his mother was looking at her with such interest.

'Would you like to meet Dell?' he asked his parents.

'We would, very much so,' said his father. 'But first we need to tell you something important. News that we ask you not to share yet with the rest of the family. Come outside so we can talk with you in private.'

Dell was enjoying herself immensely. Alex's extended family were so warm and hospitable she hadn't felt once she was an outsider. In fact she had been embraced by them because she was his friend.

A lot of good food and wine was being consumed. No wine for her of course—she hadn't touched a drop since she'd discovered she was pregnant. She realised her abstinence was probably a dead giveaway but came up with an explanation that she was allergic to alcohol. Whether or not she was believed she wasn't sure.

She looked around for Alex. Despite what half the room seemed to think, she wasn't there as Alex's date. Still, it seemed odd that he would leave her so long by herself when he was aware she only knew a handful of people.

Several times she looked around the room but didn't see him. When the older couple he had been speaking with came in by themselves, she went outside to see if she could find him.

Night had fallen and light from the *taverna* spilled out onto the beach. Some distance away, Alex stood by himself on the foreshore staring out to sea. In the semi-darkness he looked solitary and, Dell thought, sad. He had every good reason to be sad in his life but she hoped from their conversation the previous week that he was beginning to come to terms with the tragedy that had brought him to Greece. He appeared so lost in his thoughts he didn't seem aware of her approach.

Softly, Dell called his name. Startled, he turned quickly, too quickly to hide the anguish on his face.

Shocked, Dell hurried to his side. 'Alex. What's wrong? Are you okay?'

Slowly he shook his head. 'Everything is wrong.'

The devastation in his voice shocked her. 'What do you mean?'

'My parents are here. You might have seen me talking to them earlier. A surprise visit, to share some news with me, they said. But the news was to tell me my father has cancer.' His voice broke on the last words.

'Oh, Alex.' After the tragedy he'd endured he didn't deserve this. 'Is it…serious?'

'Cancer of the oesophagus. He's started radiation therapy already. More treatment when he returns to Sydney.' He clenched his fists by his sides. 'Dad is a doctor. Yet when he started having difficulty swallowing he didn't realise it could be something bad. By the time he sought help the cancer was established. There…there's a good chance he won't make it.'

Dell put her hand on his arm. 'I'm so, so sorry. Is there anything I can do to help?'

'Actually there is,' he said.

'Just tell me, fire away,' she said.

'My father told me his greatest wish is to see his only son married before he…before he dies. My mother wants it too.'

Dell gasped. 'How can I help you with that? Find you a bride?' Her words were flippant but she couldn't let him see how devastated she was at the thought of him getting married.

'My mother has already suggested a bride.'

'But…but you don't want to get married.'

'I know,' he said. 'But it's my father's dying wish. I have no choice but to consider it.'

Dell dropped her hand from his arm and stepped back, staggering a little at the pain his words stabbed into her. She struggled for the right words to show her sympathy for the situation he found himself in without revealing her hurt that he would be so insensitive as to discuss a potential bride with her.

'An arranged marriage? Didn't they go out of fashion some time ago? And what has that got to do with me?'

'Not an arranged marriage. I would never agree to such a thing. But if I chose to get married to fulfil my father's wish, the obvious bride for me is you.'

CHAPTER FIFTEEN

DELL STARED AT Alex, scarcely able to believe she'd heard his words correctly. '*Me!* Why would you say that?'

'You know how much I like and respect you, Dell. That's the first reason.'

Why did *like* and *respect* sound like the booby prizes? She wanted so much more from Alex than that. Not *love*. Of course not love, it would be way too soon for that even if insurmountable barriers didn't stand in their way. She was certainly not *in love* with Alex. A crush on her boss didn't mean she was in love with him. Of course it didn't. But she would like some passion and desire to sit there alongside *like* and *respect*. Especially if it was in regard to marriage—though this didn't sound like any marriage proposal she'd ever heard about or even imagined.

'And the other reasons?' she said faintly.

'My mother, my aunt, my cousins—even my father—assume because you're pregnant that I will do the honourable thing and marry you.'

'*What?*' The word exploded from her. 'You can't possibly be serious.'

Alex looked down into her face. Even in the slanted light from the *taverna* she could see the intensity in his black eyes. 'I'm very serious. I think we should get married.'

Dell had never known what it felt to have her head spin. She felt it now. Alex had to take hold of her elbow to steady her. 'I can't believe I'm hearing this,' she said. 'You said you'd never get married. I'm not pregnant to you. In fact you see my pregnancy as a barrier to kissing me, let alone marrying me. Have you been drinking too much ouzo?'

'Not a drop,' he said. 'It's my father's dying wish that I get married. He's been a good father. I haven't been a good son. Fulfilling that wish is important to me. If I have to get married, it makes sense that I marry you.'

'It doesn't make a scrap of sense to me,' she said. 'You don't get married to someone to please someone else, even if it is your father.'

Alex frowned. 'You've misunderstood me. I'm not talking about a real marriage.'

This was getting more and more surreal. 'Not a real marriage? You mean a marriage of convenience?'

'Yes. Like people do to be able to get residence in a country. In this case it would be marriage to make my father happy. He wants the peace of mind of seeing me settled.'

'You feel you owe your father?'

'I owe him so much it could never be calculated or repaid. This isn't about owing my father, it's about loving him. I love my father, Dell.'

But you'll never love me, she cried in her heart. How could he talk about marrying someone—anyone—without a word about love?

'I'm so sorry, Alex, about your father's illness. But perhaps the shock of his sad news has skewed your thinking. Perhaps it has even…unhinged you,' she said. 'Who would think such a sudden marriage is in any way reasonable or sensible?'

'My family would not question marriage to you. In fact I believe they think us getting married is virtually a *fait accompli.*'

Dell was too astounded by his reasoning to be able to reply. She fought to keep her voice under control when she did. 'What about me? Where do I fit in this decision-making process? Aren't I entitled to an opinion?'

He put up his hand to placate her. 'You're right. I'm sorry. It seemed like such a good idea and I've rushed things. You know often my best decisions are made on impulse.' She had become so knowledgeable about his business dealings she had to admit the truth of that.

'This is my life we're talking about here, Alex. I deserve more than a rushed decision.'

'When it comes to your life, I think you'll see it makes a lot of sense,' he said.

'Please enlighten me,' she said. 'I'm still not

convinced I'm not dealing with an idea sprung from grief-stricken madness.'

He shook his head but it was more a gesture of annoyance that he should be so misunderstood than anything else. 'Let me explain my perfectly sane thoughts,' he said.

'I'm listening,' she said, intrigued.

'You help me with this and there are benefits to you. You'll be able to stay here to have your baby, surrounded by people who will no longer be strangers. I have dual nationality so you would be the wife of a Greek citizen. Your baby will have a name. And I will support him or her until he or she is twenty-one years of age. You wouldn't have to ask your parents any favours or perjure yourself to get government social security. In fact you would be able to enjoy the rest of your pregnancy and after the birth without worrying about money or finding a place to live. And I imagine it would be somewhat satisfying to stick it up the BX.'

His last point dragged a smile from her. Clever Alex with his charisma and business smarts made the crazy scheme seem reasonable. But there must be more to it than that, an ulterior motive.

'It would also get the media off your back regarding Mia,' she said. 'Quite the fairy-tale romance. The press would lap it up. The story would make great publicity for your new venture.' She couldn't keep the cynical note from her voice. 'I suppose you've considered that angle.'

Alex stilled. 'Actually, I haven't. You can't honestly think that's a consideration?'

'I'm hardly privy to your thoughts,' she said.

'My only motivation here is my father's happiness while he's battling cancer. Since Mia's death I've done my best to make reparation to the people I harmed with my aggressive business techniques and ruthless selfishness. People like you. I'll never get the chance to make amends for my behaviour towards Mia and I'll live with that for the rest of my life. But I can try to make up for it with my father by getting married so he can dance at my wedding before he dies.'

If Alex had said just one thing about how fond he was of her, and for that reason if he was going to have to marry someone he would want it to be her, Dell would probably have burst into tears and said she'd do it. But he didn't. So she toughened her attitude.

She remembered how she'd felt when he'd kissed her at the Parthenon. How exciting it had been, how happy being in his arms had made her. How she'd ached for more.

'You say it wouldn't be a real marriage. I guess that means no…well, no sex.'

'That's right,' he said, so quickly it was hurtful. 'That wouldn't be fair to you when our bargain would have an end.'

As if it wouldn't be fair to bind her to a sexless, loveless union with a man who even now in this cold-blooded conversation made her long to be close to him—both physically and every other way. It would be a cruel kind of torture.

'What do you mean "our bargain"?' she asked. Thoughts about his proposition spun round and round in her mind.

'This would all be done legally. I would get my lawyers to draw up a contract setting out the terms and conditions. How you and your baby would be recompensed. The marriage would be of one year's duration.' His face contorted with anguish. 'Less if…if my father were to die before then.'

A great wave of compassion for him swept through her. He had been through so much. 'Oh, Alex, is it that bad?'

Her instinct was to comfort him, to put her arms around him, to try and take some of his pain for herself. But she kept her hands by her sides. This was not the moment for that.

He nodded, seemingly unable to speak. 'It seems so.'

They were already standing very close to each other without being conscious of it. The nature of the exchange of conversation needed to be for their ears only. A cool breeze ruffled her hair and made her shiver.

He put his hand on her shoulder. In the semi-light he looked more handsome than ever, more unattainable. The stronger his connection to his family grew, the more Greek he seemed to become. 'Please, Dell. I think we've become friends of a kind. If you don't want to agree to this for the very real benefits to you, can you do it as an act of friendship? I'll make sure you won't regret it. Please say yes. Please marry me. There isn't anyone else I'd rather be getting on board with this than you.'

Was that a subtle reminder that he was so determined to do this that if she said no, he'd find another woman who would jump at the chance to be the make-believe bride of multimillionaire Alex Mikhalis?

Could she bear it if he married someone else?

She took a deep breath. 'Yes, Alex, I say yes.'

His sigh of relief was audible, even on the beach with the muted music and chatter coming from the *taverna*, the swish of the small waves as they rolled up onto the tiny pebbles on the beach. 'Thank you, Dell. You won't regret this, I promise you.'

Already she knew she would regret it. Everything about the arrangement seemed so wrong. On top of that, she was tired of putting on her fluffy-chick face, of pretending she was happy when she wasn't. Now she had signed up for a year of pretending that she didn't care about the man who was going to be her fake husband in a marriage of convenience.

'I guess I'd be working for you, still. A different job. A new contract.' She tried to sound pragmatic, to justify the unjustifiable.

Alex frowned. 'I hadn't thought of it like that.'

'It might make it easier if we did.'

'Perhaps,' he said, sounding unconvinced. He took a step closer.

'But right now I need you to kiss me.'

'What?'

His gaze flickered over her shoulder and back to face her. 'You can't see from where you're standing but there are interested eyes on us. In theory I just proposed to you and you said "yes". A kiss is appropriate.'

Appropriate? When was a kiss *appropriate*? Obviously in this alternate universe she had agreed to enter the rules were very different. That didn't mean she had to abide by them.

She looked up at his dark eyes, his sensual mouth she ached to kiss in an entirely inappropriate way. 'I've got a better idea. *You* can kiss *me*. And you'd better make it look believable.'

Dell was challenging him. Alex had been exultant that she had acquiesced to his admittedly unconventional plan. But it seemed Dell and acquiescence didn't go hand in hand. Somehow, in a contrary kind of way, that pleased him. Dell wouldn't be Dell if she rolled over and did just as he commanded.

It made him want to kiss her for real.

Her eyes glittered in the soft half-light, tiny flecks of gold among the green. Her lips were slightly parted, a hint of a smile lifting the corners—halfway between teasing and seductive. 'What are you waiting for?' she murmured.

He was very aware of their audience. The family members who must have watched her seek him out on the beach. They stood inside the doorway some twenty metres away, obviously thinking they couldn't be seen, but the lights from the *taverna* highlighted their shapes. It appeared the group had gathered hoping, perhaps, for proof that he and Dell were a couple. He would give them that proof.

He pulled her to him and pressed his mouth to hers with a firm, gentle pressure. In reply, Dell wound her arms around his neck to pull his head closer, her curves moulded against him. Her scent sent an intoxicating rush to his head— the sharpness of lemon and thyme soap mingled with her own sweet womanliness. It was a scent so familiar to his senses he was instantly aware of when she entered or left a room. She kissed him back, then flicked the tip of her tongue between his lips with a little murmur deep in her throat. Surprise quickly turned to enthusiastic response as he met her tongue with his, deepening the kiss, falling into a vortex of sensation.

Alex forgot he was on the beach, forgot they had an audience, forgot everything but that Dell was in his arms and he was kissing her. This was no meandering journey between gentle kiss of affirmation and one of full-blown passion. It raced there like a lit fuse on a stick of dynamite. Lips, tongues, teeth met and danced together in an escalating rhythm. Desire burned through him, and her too, judging by her response as that little murmur of appreciation intensified into a moan. He groaned his own want in reply, pulled her close, as close as they could be with their clothes between them. He could feel the hammering of her heart against his chest. His hands slid down her waist to cup the cheeks of her bottom; she pushed closer as she fiercely kissed him.

'Get a room, you two.' Cristos's voice, in Greek, pierced his consciousness.

Dell pulled away. 'What was that?' Her cheeks were flushed, her breath coming in gasps, her mouth pink and swollen from his kisses.

Alex had trouble finding his own voice, had to drag in air to control his breathing.

'My cousin trying to be funny,' he said.

She looked up at him, her breasts rising and

falling as she struggled to get her breath. 'Alex…
that was—'

'I know,' he said, not certain of how it happened, knowing what it meant for their bargain,
realising he had lost control and that he had to
take back the lead.

Her eyes met his as a shadow behind them
dimmed their brightness. 'We can't do that. A
kiss like that wasn't what you'd call *appropriate*. It wasn't fair. Not when I—'

When she *what*? Alex wanted, needed, to
know what she meant. Because at that moment
when she had moaned her desire something had
shifted for him. Something deep and fundamen-
tal and perplexing. He had to know if she had
felt it too.

But there was no chance to ask her. Because
then his family, headed by his parents, were
spilling out of the *taverna* onto the beach and
surrounding them with exclamations of surprise
and glee and, from his mother, joy.

'I knew from the moment I saw them together,

they were more than friends,' he heard Aunt Penelope explain. Not explain—*gloat.*

He looked down at Dell, who looked as though she had been well and truly kissed. In a silent question, he raised his brow; she affirmed with a silent nod.

He put his arm around her. It wasn't difficult to fake possessiveness. 'Dell has just agreed to marry me,' he announced.

There was an explosion of congratulations and laughter. He looked up to see mingled pride, relief and love on his father's face.

'Thank you, Dell,' Alex whispered to her. 'I won't forget what you're doing for me and my family.'

Her face closed. 'It's just a business arrangement between us, remember,' she whispered back, being very careful she wouldn't be overheard.

So she hadn't felt it. He knew he had no right to feel disappointed. Nevertheless, his mood darkened but he had to keep up with the momentum of excitement as he and Dell were swept back into the *taverna*.

The third time someone wished them *'I ora I kali'* Dell turned to ask him what it meant. 'It means, "May the wedding day come soon",' he replied. 'And we need to have it as soon as possible. My father needs to get back to Sydney to continue his treatment. Is that okay with you?'

She shrugged. 'You're the boss. But of course it's okay with me. The sooner the better really.'

'You have made me very happy, son,' his father said when he reached them. 'Dell, welcome to our family.'

That made it worth it.

His mother burst into tears. 'Of joy, these are tears of joy,' she said, fanning her face with both hands. 'Dell, I've heard so many good things about you I feel I know you already.' She gave another sob. 'And my son looks so happy. Happier than since…well, you know what happened.'

Dell looked to him for help, started to stutter a response but he was saved by his cousin Melina who had helped him with her contacts in

Athens. She picked up Dell's left hand. 'Show us your engagement ring, Dell,' she said.

A ring.

He hadn't thought of that.

It was immediately obvious that Dell's hand was bare. She shot a look of panic to him.

'This all happened very quickly,' he said. 'I will be—'

His mother saved him by sliding off a ring, sparkling with a large diamond, from her own left hand and handing it to him. 'Take this. Your father bought it for me for our anniversary a few years back. Our own engagement ring is something much more humble, bought when we were both students.'

She shared a glance of such love with his father, Alex felt stricken. Was faking his own marriage really the way to do this? But there was no going back now.

He took the ring and slid it onto the third finger of Dell's left hand. Her hand was trembling as she held it up for his family's inspection. There was a roar of approval. 'I will get you your own engagement ring, of course,' he said to her.

'That would be the height of hypocrisy and totally unnecessary,' she murmured, smiling for their audience as though she were whispering something romantic. 'You can give this ring back to your mother when our agreement is over.'

To anyone but him, who had got to know her so well over the last weeks, Dell seemed to accept the exuberant hugs and congratulations with happiness and an appropriate touch of bewilderment at how fast things had moved. However he noticed signs of strain around her mouth, a slightly glazed look in her eyes that told him how she was struggling to keep up the façade.

He did the only thing he could do to mask her face from his family. He swept her into his arms and kissed her again. And again for good measure because he didn't want to stop.

Dell was tired, bone weary. Her face hurt from so much forced smiling and acceptance of congratulations. Aunt Penelope's birthday party had turned into a shared celebration to include an informal engagement party for her and Alex. She felt ill-prepared for the wave of jubilation that had picked her up and carried her into the heart of his Greek family.

She had long realised the truth that Greek people were among the most hospitable in the world. Their generosity of welcome to her now stepped up a level because she was going to be part of the family. There was a certain amount of unsaid *I told you so* that, even in her fear of saying the wrong thing and inadvertently revealing the truth about her engagement, made her smile.

One thing came through loud and clear—Alex was well loved by everyone. She heard of his many acts of quiet generosity, the hard work he'd put into family projects. Even the children, who were very much part of the celebration, seemed to adore him, flocking around him. He leaned down to listen very gravely to what one little cherub with a mop of black curls and baby black eyes was saying to him. The toddler could have been his own son. Her heart turned over and she felt very strongly the presence of the baby in her womb. Should Alex have thought more about this plan before sweeping her up into it? Should she have done the sensible thing and said *no*?

It also became obvious how deeply worried his family had been about him. His father, George, explained how, after the siege in Alex's restaurant, he had feared his son had been heading for a breakdown. How desperately concerned he and Eleni, his wife, had been about him. How happy they were that their son had found some measure of peace back in the homeland of his grandfather's family. 'And now this, the best news we could have.'

Eleni patted her hand. 'To marry into a big Greek family can be overwhelming, I know. I will do anything I can to help you. Will your own mother be here?'

Her own parents. What would she say to them? More secrets and lies. 'I'm not sure they'll be able to make the wedding at such short notice.' Her astute mother would realise immediately all was not as it should be. It wasn't a real marriage; she was tempted not to tell her parents about it at all.

'That would be a shame,' Eleni said, trying to hide her obvious shock that the bride's mother would not be in attendance.

Dell tried to play it down. 'Did Alex tell you I've been married before? I'm divorced. It's why we want to have a very simple civil ceremony.'

'He did mention it,' Eleni said. 'But it is his first wedding. I can't understand why he wants so little fuss made.' Dell wasn't surprised by the familiar female gaze as it dropped to her middle. 'Although we do understand the need to get married quickly.'

Dell refused to bite. 'George's treatment. Of course, I understand you need to get back to Sydney.'

Just then Aunt Penelope bustled up to take Dell's arm. Dell was immediately aware of an unspoken rivalry between Penelope and Eleni of the *I found her first* variety. Penelope pointed out that the matter of her wedding dress needed immediate attention. A lovely gown was not something that could be made overnight. Dell needed to think about it straight away. And her friend, a dressmaker, happened to be a guest at the party; she should meet her now.

'I'd thought I'd buy a dress off the rack in Athens,' Dell said, casting a helpless call for intervention to the more sophisticated Eleni.

Aunt Penelope didn't miss a thing. 'Ah, you think a village dressmaker could not make you the kind of wedding dress you want? My friend used to work in a bridal couture house in Athens. You show her a picture in any wedding magazine or on the Internet and she can make it for you.' As she led Dell away she added in a low murmur, 'My friend will help you choose the best style to accommodate your bump and allow for the dress to be let out if we need to do so in the days before the wedding.'

Dell stared at Alex's great-aunt, not sure what to say. Penelope laughed. 'You won't be the first Mikhalis bride to have a baby come earlier than expected after the wedding.'

Later, when she and Alex grabbed a quiet moment together Dell told him what had happened. 'Why didn't anyone tell me Aunt Penelope used to be a midwife? She told me she has delivered hundreds, maybe thousands, of babies and that she knew immediately I was pregnant that first day I went to the doctor. How are we going to tell them that the baby isn't yours?'

'We won't,' he said as he got swept away from her by the men to take part in the traditional male dances, some of them unique to these islands, that were an important part of any celebration.

As she watched Alex, as adept as any of the men in the dance, she knew she was there in this happy celebration under completely false pretences. Alex's motivations were worthy but how would these warm, wonderful people feel when they found out they'd been fooled?

Secrets and lies.

The most difficult secret for her to hide was her growing feelings for Alex and the most difficult lie was one she had to tell herself—that she didn't wish, somewhere deep in her heart, that this engagement party and the wedding that would follow as soon as they could arrange it were for real and she really was his much-loved bride.

CHAPTER SIXTEEN

TO GET MARRIED in a hurry in Greece involved more paperwork than Dell had imagined, especially when Alex was being wed to a divorced foreigner. Then there had been issues with the venue. In Australia, you could get married anywhere you wanted by a civil celebrant. Not so in Greece. For a civil ceremony there was no choice but to get married in a town hall. The paperwork had been pushed through, expedited by the right people, so they were able to get married. But no one in Alex's family had been happy at the prospect of what they saw as a bland, meaningless civil union.

Before Dell knew it the ancient, tiny white chapel on Kosmimo had been re-consecrated and, two weeks after their impromptu 'engagement', she and Alex were getting the church wedding his family had clamoured for.

This was her not-for-real wedding day and she was feeling nervous. She had not spent much time alone with Alex in the past two weeks. The day after the party for Aunt Penelope, she had moved off Kosmimo and back to the villa. Her morning sickness was practically gone—though the weariness persisted—and the daily boat trips to the island and back to Nidri were bearable. Alex's family didn't think it appropriate they should be living on the island together so close to the wedding.

Dell might have put up an argument about that but in truth it was a relief. She hadn't been able to endure the close proximity to Alex sharing the pavilion with him. It was torture wanting him, knowing she couldn't have him.

She'd repeatedly reminded herself that the marriage was just a business deal. Another employment contract signed with the hospitality tycoon. It was the only way she could retain some measure of sanity among the excitement generated by his family, as they planned the wedding of their beloved son, nephew, cousin, to the Australian girlfriend they had given their seal of approval.

No one seemed to think it was unusual that the engaged couple had so little time together. George and Eleni had moved on to Kosmimo into one of the finished guestrooms. Understandably, Alex wanted to spend as much time as he could with his parents. Dell was always included and she did her best to be affectionate with Alex without anyone suspecting that her edginess was anything but pre-wedding nerves. She tried to hold herself a little aloof from George and Eleni because she really liked them. They were every bit as intelligent as her parents but in a warm, inclusive way. Losing them at the end of the year as well as Alex would be an added level of pain; the thought of losing George earlier was unbearable. Thank heaven she'd agreed to help Alex in his audacious plan.

She didn't have to feign interest in Alex's parents' stories and reminiscences of him as a little boy and rebellious teenager. She lapped up every detail and realised her obvious fascination with everything to do with her husband-to-be was noted and approved. George and Eleni, Aunt Penelope and Uncle Stavros made their delight in his choice of bride only too apparent. If Alex's kisses, staged in sight of some observant family member, got a tad too enthusiastic she was only too happy to go along with them. All in the interests of authenticity.

Two days ago, while working alone with Alex in their office on Kosmimo, she had felt a bubbling sensation in her womb and cried out. Alex had jumped up from his desk and rushed to her. 'What's wrong?' he'd said.

Then with sudden joy she'd realised. 'It's the baby moving inside me.' She'd put her hand on her small bump, waited, and felt the tiniest ripple of movement. 'My baby is kicking, I think.' She'd forgotten all about the complex layers of her relationship with Alex and just wanted to share this momentous discovery with him.

Alex had stood in front of her and she'd realised he was lost for words, a gamut of emotions rippling across his face. She'd been amazed to see shyness and a kind of wonder predominate. 'May I...may I feel it?' he'd finally asked.

Silently she'd taken his hand and placed it on her bump, her hand resting on top of his. The little tremor had come again. Then again. Alex had kept his hand there. When he'd spoken, his voice had been tinged with awe. 'There's a little person in there. Maybe a future football player with a kick like that.'

She'd smiled through sudden tears that had threatened to spill. 'Yes. There really, truly is. My little boy or girl. The baby I've wanted for so long.' Happiness had welled through her. The moment with Alex had been a moment so precious, so unexpected that she'd found herself not daring to say anything further, not wanting to break the magic of it.

Alex had been the first to end the silence between them. His hand had slipped from her bump and he had taken both her hands in his. 'Dell, I know this is something that I—' he'd started. But she never heard what he'd intended to say as the man tiling the kitchens had knocked on the door with a query for Alex.

The by now familiar shutters had come down over Alex's eyes, he'd dropped her hands and stepped back to turn and deal with the tiler, leaving her confused and shaken.

Now she stood at the entrance to the little chapel, in the most picturesque setting she could imagine near the edge of a cliff with perfect blue skies above and the rippling turquoise sea below.

The ceremony was to be a contemporary one, in recognition of the Australian background of both the bride and groom. But there would also be the traditional Greek Orthodox wedding service. She had been walked up from the resort to the chapel by her attendants, Alex's two sisters and his cousin Melina from Athens. His sisters had flown in yesterday from Sydney, husbands and children in tow. Aunt Penelope had organised dresses for all three as well as Melina's sweet little daughter, who had walked ahead strewing rose petals.

It was purely a Mikhalis family occasion and Dell was okay about that. This wasn't about her. It was about Alex and his love and loyalty for his father and her chance to help him right one of the wrongs he imagined he'd caused people close to him.

So here she was, surrounded by so much goodwill and happiness it was palpable, like a wave rushing through the wedding party and guests and whirling them around in its wake. But it was based on a false premise: that she was about to become Alex's loving wife and the mother of his child.

She was a fraud.

Could it be any wonder that, as she took her first steps over the threshold of the chapel, she was the most miserable she had ever been in her life? Her happy-chick face was threatening to crack from overuse. She took a deep breath to try and control her fear of the wrong she was about to do to this family and it came out as a gasp. Immediately friendly, comforting hands were upon her, patting down and soothing what they so obviously saw as a case of bride-to-be jitters.

She couldn't do this.

Then another step took her inside and she saw Alex waiting by the side of the small stone altar that had been festooned by his family with flowers. Her heart seemed to stop. He had never looked more handsome, his black hair and olive skin in striking contrast to his white linen suit. But it was the look of admiration and pride on his face as he caught sight of her that set her heart racing. It wasn't *love*, she knew that, but it was enough to let her decide to rip off that mask she was so weary of wearing and show him how she really felt. Later, she could put it down to what a good actress she had been on the day.

But right now she was going to let the truth shine from her eyes.

She loved him.

The person she had lied to the most was herself. Because she loved Alex Mikhalis with all her heart and soul and she could no longer deny it. She realised this was a make-believe wedding and nothing more would come of it but she was going to behave as though this were her real wedding.

To pretend just for this day there was love and a future.

She smiled back at him, a tremulous smile that she knew revealed her heart completely without artifice. Their gazes connected and held and there was no one else in that tiny church but her and the man she loved. But she could not tell him how deeply and passionately she felt all those things a make-believe bride should not feel for her pretend husband. There would be heartbreak enough when their contract came to an end— one way or another.

Dell in her wedding dress was so breathtakingly beautiful that Alex found himself clenching his hands by his sides in an agony of suppressed emotion. He wasn't aware of anyone or anything else. Not his father and his cousin Cristos by his side. Not the priest behind them. Not the tiny church filled with his Greek family and friends, the scent of roses and a lingering trace of incense, the sound of the sea breaking on the limestone rocks beneath. All his senses were filled by the beauty of the bride walking slowly towards him. *His* bride.

She was wearing an exquisite long dress of fine silk and lace, deceptively simple, cleverly draped to hide the secret everyone seemed to be only too aware of. Her hair was pulled back from her face and entwined with flowers at the nape of her neck and he knew the gown swooped low at the back and finished with a flat bow. She carried a bouquet of white roses and tiny white daisies, the traditional gift of the groom to his bride. Pearl earrings from her new mother-in-law hung from her ears.

He knew the whole wedding was a sham, although created with the best of intentions. But suddenly he ached for this marriage of convenience to be a marriage of the heart. For Dell to be his wife for real. As she took her place next to him and the traditional crowns connected by ribbons were placed on first her head and then on his, the realisation hit him.

She was his wings.

Dell was the one who would help him soar back into the full happiness and joy of life. Without her he would still be grounded, plodding along looking backwards and sideward, sometimes forward but never up to the sky where he longed to be. But he couldn't soar to great heights unless she was by his side. He needed her. *He loved her.*

How blind he'd been, how barricaded against ever finding love, ever thinking he *deserved* love that he hadn't seen it when love had found him. When had he fallen for her? At Bay Breeze when she'd been so kind at a time she'd had every reason to hate him? Or the day she'd zoomed up on her bike so full of life and vitality shining her own brand of brightness into his dark, shadowed life? Whenever it had been, he realised now that the job offer, the move to Greece had all been an excuse to have her nearby.

He had to tell her how he felt.

How ironic they were repeating vows—in Greek and in English—to bind their lives together. Desperately he tried to infuse all his longing and love for her into their vows, hoping she would sense it, wanting this to be the one and only time he ever made these vows. Vows that made her his lifetime partner. When they were pronounced man and wife he kissed her with a fierce longing surely she must have felt. Then searched her face for a hint of returned feeling, exulting when he saw it, plunging into despair when he realised it could be all part of the game of pretence he had lured her into playing.

But telling her how he felt wasn't possible in a snatched aside between the rounds of congratulations and the endless photos. Then when they walked down the hill to the new resort he had created with her, where the party was to be held, they had to face the reception line that saw them individually greeting their guests.

He felt a pang of regret and sorrow when he

realised she had none of her own family and friends there. She had point-blank refused to involve them in what she called the big lie. In all conscience he had not attempted to convince her otherwise. Now he wished he had done what he had wanted to do in the interests of authenticity—gone behind her back and invited her parents and Lizzie and Jesse. Because he didn't intend for her ever to have another wedding—this was it, for him and for her. He had every intention of claiming her for his bride for real.

After the feasting and the speeches, and before the dancing would begin, he managed to lead her out to the marble balcony that looked out over the sea. When a guest with a camera tried to follow them out he gestured for her to leave him alone with his new wife. He and Dell watched her depart and saw her tell others that the bride and groom needed some time together.

Alone with her, Alex found himself behaving like a stuttering adolescent. 'It went well,' he said. Of all things to come out when he had so much he wanted to say. Life-changing words, not inane chit-chat.

'Yes,' she said with a wistfulness he hadn't seen before in her and that nourished the glimmer of hope he'd felt at the church. 'I…I think we managed to…to fool everyone.' Fool them? Fool *him*? 'We both put on quite an act.' *An act?* Was that really all it was for her?

'Dell, did you…did you find yourself during the ceremony wanting…?' Where were his usual eloquent words when he wanted them?

Her brow pleated in a frown. 'Wanting what?'

Wanting our vows to be real. The words hovered on his tongue. But she seemed so cool and contained. What would he do if she denied any feeling for him? He had a year to convince her. He shouldn't rush into this—it was too important for him to get wrong. 'Wanting your family to be there?' he finished lamely.

There were shadows behind her eyes when she looked up at him. Her mouth twisted downwards. 'No, I didn't. There are going to be enough people disappointed and hurt when they find out the truth of what this wedding meant—or didn't mean. I don't want my side dragged into it.'

Her voice wasn't steady and he realised how difficult the deception was for her honest nature, how, although his father was beaming with happiness, perhaps his plan had not been in Dell's best interest. But how very different it might be if their marriage was for real. He had the crazy idea of proposing to her in earnest out here on the balcony. Going down on bended knee. But he thought about it for a moment too long.

She turned away from him, her shoulders slumped before she pulled them back up straight. 'We'd better get back to our guests. Act Three of this performance is about to start—the dancing.' Then she turned back, lifted her face to his in the offer of a kiss. 'We'd better do what our guests will expect us to do, Alex, a husband and wife alone together for the first time.'

When her cool lips met his, he knew she was pretending and he didn't like the feeling one bit. As she moved away he saw the moment she pasted a smile on her face and forced a brightness to her eyes he knew she didn't feel. Making her his bride for real might be more difficult than he had anticipated.

CHAPTER SEVENTEEN

LEAVING HER DISASTROUS encounter with Alex on the balcony, Dell retreated to the bathroom—the only place she could get a few moments to herself. She splashed her face with cool water, being careful not to damage her make-up. There would be more photos to come and she still had to play her role of the happy bride.

Back in the beautiful little church on the cliff-top, there had been no need for her to pretend. After the fervent way Alex had repeated his marriage vows, not taking his eyes from hers for a second, her heart had done a dance of joy, convinced he might feel towards her something of what she felt towards him. And that kiss… He had really taken the invitation to kiss his bride to the extreme. Her toes in her kitten-heeled satin shoes curled at the memory of it. No wonder the congregation had applauded them.

But on the balcony his stilted conversation had proved anything but satisfactory. How foolish she had been to let the romance of an extravagant wedding catch her off her guard. And yet... For a moment she'd been convinced he had something important to say. Maybe he had thought it was important to talk about the fact her family wasn't there. But was it because he'd thought it mattered to her or because it might make people question the authenticity of their marriage?

She closed her eyes and let a wave of weariness wash over her. Actually, she'd let her personal feelings overcome her business sense. When her carefully worded press release went out announcing Alex's marriage and the news got out, people might question the lack of participation by her family in the wedding. She'd have to think of a way to explain it. So maybe that was what Alex had been trying to say. But she felt too tired to worry about that just yet. Not just tired. Unwell. She smoothed back her hair from her face and prepared to return to the fray.

Then the cramp hit her. And another. She clutched her stomach protectively. Saw her face go white in the mirror.

Please, not that, not now.

But when she went into the stall to check, there was blood.

Dell rested her face in her hands. Her baby was kicking. She'd allowed herself to believe everything was all right. This couldn't be happening. She couldn't get up, couldn't move, frozen with terror and disbelief and grief.

She didn't know for how long she sat there. But there was a knock on the door. 'Are you all right in there, Dell?'

Aunt Penelope. The woman who had been so good to her since she had arrived in Greece. She was a midwife. Aunt Penelope would know what to do. Dell opened the door.

'The baby?' the older woman asked.

Dell nodded. And let herself be looked after by her new family who weren't really her family at all.

Alex was talking to his cousin Melina about her four-year-old daughter who was their delightful flower girl. He hadn't even known Melina had a child until quite recently. Melina was explaining when his father interrupted them. Alex knew something was wrong when his father tapped him on the arm and took him aside. Dell needed to be taken to hospital urgently. She wasn't well and there was a chance she could be miscarrying. He heard the cry of anguish before realising it was his.

But his father told him he needed to be strong. How much had he had to drink because his speedboat was the fastest way to get his wife off the island? Fortunately all he'd had was a flute of champagne.

His wife.

Alex found Dell surrounded by the women in his family. His aunt, his mother, his sisters. She looked ashen, her eyes fearful, her hair falling in disarray around her face, stripped of her wedding gown and wearing the white dress with the blue tie she'd worn when he'd first kissed her in front of the Parthenon.

But when they saw him, the women stepped back so he could gather her in his arms. She collapsed against him and he could feel her trembling. 'Alex, I'm scared.'

'I know you are, *agapi mou*,' he said, scarcely realising he had used the Greek endearment for *darling*. 'Try not to worry. We're getting you to the hospital as fast as we can.' He knew how important this baby was to her. He would do anything he could to help her.

Alex murmured a constant litany of reassurance as he picked Dell up and carried her out of the building and down the steps leading to the water. But still he hadn't told her how much he loved her.

She protested she could walk but he wasn't taking any chances. He carried her to the dock where his boat, and the boats that had brought over the guests, were moored.

Then the women took over again as he took the wheel, released the throttle and pointed the boat towards Lefkada. People were worried about the baby. He was too. Since the day he had felt it move the baby had become real to him. But he was racked with the terrible fear that something might happen to Dell. He had a sickening sense of history repeating itself. Would he lose Dell as he'd lost Mia with her believing he didn't care about her?

The next morning, Dell lay drowsing in the hospital bed, hooked up to a number of monitors. She felt a change, sensed a familiar scent. When she opened her eyes it was to see Alex sprawled in a chair that had been pulled over by her bedside. He was still wearing his wedding suit, crumpled now, and his jaw was dark with stubble. Even dishevelled he was gorgeous. He wore a wide gold band on his right hand in the

Greek manner. The ring that was meant to bind him to her.

Her ring—his mother's ring—was sitting tightly wrapped in her handbag inside the hospital cabinet. She would never wear it again.

'You're awake,' he said, his voice gruff.

'Yes,' she said.

'I didn't think you were ever going to wake up.' She hadn't been asleep the entire time. But she'd requested no visitors. Not even her husband. Until now.

He went to kiss her but she pushed back against her pillow to evade him. 'No need for that. There's no one here we need to fool.' Was that hurt she saw tighten his face? Surely not. She wanted his kiss, *ached* for his kiss. But she needed to keep her distance more.

'I'm sorry about our honeymoon,' she said. 'Have you managed to cancel the booking?' For appearances' sake, they had planned a short break in the old port town of Chania on the southern island of Crete.

His dark brows drew together. 'Why would

I care about that when I'm worried sick about you? I haven't slept for fearing something would happen to you. And the baby.'

His reference to the baby surprised her. 'I'm okay,' she said. 'I don't want a fuss. I'm not miscarrying.'

He let out his breath on a great sigh of relief. 'Thank God. Are you sure about that?'

'Yes,' she said. 'But I need to stay in bed for a few days.'

She didn't want to discuss the intimate details with him. They hadn't been intimate. Hadn't made this baby together. It was nothing to do with him. As he'd made so very clear on several occasions.

He leaned closer to her. She could smell coffee on his breath. Noticed his eyes were bloodshot. 'Do you have to stay in hospital?' he asked. 'Or can you come home to Kosmima? I can organise nursing care for you.'

Home. The island wasn't home for her. Much as she had come to love it.

She took a deep breath to steady herself, braced

herself against the pillows. 'I'm not coming back to Kosmima, Alex. Not today. Not ever.'

She expected him to be angry but he looked puzzled. Which made this so much harder. 'You want to go back to the villa? Why? That's not part of our agreement.'

'Not the villa. I'm going back to Sydney.'

'*What?*' The word exploded from him.

Slowly she shook her head. 'I can't do this, Alex. I'm reneging on our agreement. I'm sorry but I just can't live a lie. Your family are so wonderful. Aunt Penelope has been like a mother to me. Your mother too. I…I've come to love them. But I'm an imposter. A fraud. They're all so worried about me losing this baby because they think it's yours. Can you imagine how they will feel when they find out the truth?'

'But we're married now.'

'In name only. It's not a legal marriage.' She couldn't meet his eye. 'It…it hasn't been consummated, for one thing.'

'That could be arranged,' he said slowly.

She caught her breath. 'I know you don't mean that,' she said.

'What if I did?'

'I wouldn't believe you,' she said. 'You've never given any indication whatsoever that... that you wanted this marriage to be real.'

'Neither have you,' he countered.

'Why would I?' she said. 'This...this marriage is a business arrangement. I've signed a contract drawn up by your lawyers.'

'A contract you would be breaking if you went back to Sydney.'

'I'm aware of that,' she said. 'But the consequences of staying with you are so much greater than anything you could do to me by pursuing the broken contract. So sue me. I have nothing.' She displayed empty hands. 'The marriage isn't registered yet. If a marriage in Greece is not registered within forty days, it becomes invalid.'

He didn't say anything in reply to that. His expression was immeasurably sad. 'So it comes full circle, does it, Dell?' he said finally. 'Are we enemies again?'

How could he be an enemy when she loved him so much her heart was breaking at the thought of not being with him? But she couldn't endure a year of living with a man she loved so desperately in a celibate, for-convenience marriage. And then be expected to walk away from it with a cheque in her pocket, never to bother him again.

'Never an enemy, Alex,' she said with a hitch to her voice.

'So why this desire to run away to Australia? Surely it's not just about my family. So we keep to our deal and we break up after a year. Divorce happens all the time.' He shrugged. 'They'll get over it.'

She glared at him. 'You don't get it. You just don't get it, do you? You can't just play around with love, anyone's love.' *My* love.

Her voice was rising but she couldn't do anything to control it. A nurse came into the room. 'Are you okay, Mrs Mikhalis? Is something upsetting you?'

The nurse looked pointedly at Alex, who stood

glowering by the chair. But Dell was too stunned at the way she'd so matter-of-factly referred to her as *Mrs Mikhalis* to really notice.

Alex towered over the hospital bed, over the hapless nurse. 'I am her husband and the father of her baby. I am not *upsetting* her. I'm here to take her home. To the people who love her.' Now he completely ignored the nurse, rather turned to face Dell. 'To the man who loves her.'

The nurse knew exactly when to exit the room quietly.

Dell pushed herself up higher in the bed. 'Was that "the man who loves her" bit for the benefit of the nurse, Alex?'

He came closer to the bed, took both her hands in his. 'It's purely for your benefit. I love you, Dell. I have for a long time. It just took me a while to wake up to it.'

'Oh, Alex, I love you too.' She gripped his hands tight. 'I…I thought I had a silly crush on you but…but it was so much more than that.'

'Aunt Penelope, the family, they saw it before we did,' he said.

He leaned down to kiss her, tenderly and with love. The same love she recognised now from his kiss in the church. Her heart started a furious pounding.

'Alex, the wedding. The vows. You meant every word, didn't you?'

'Every word. I was hoping you would recognise that.'

'I meant every word too,' she breathed. He kissed her again.

'That means we really are married,' he said. 'Registered or not. I want to take you home with me where you belong.'

'But what about the baby? You said you could never take on another man's child.'

He frowned. 'Somehow, I have never thought of the child as anyone's but yours,' he said. 'Then when I felt your baby move beneath my hand, I realised it didn't matter who was the sperm donor. The father will be the man who welcomes it into the world, who loves its mother, who truly *fathers* it, like my father fathered me.'

'That's quite a turnaround,' she said, a little breathlessly. 'Do you really believe that?'

'Our little flower girl today, you know she is adopted?'

'No, I didn't know that.'

'Neither did I, until Melina happened to mention it today. I was in Sydney at the time. She said she loved her little girl the minute she first held her in her arms. Her husband felt the same.'

'She's a very loved child, that's obvious,' Dell said thoughtfully.

'That she is. So why would I not love your child, Dell? I love you so that's halfway there. I guess I won't know how I feel exactly until I see him or her but I guess no parent does. I'll be there at the birth if you want me to and be involved from the very beginning.'

Dell put her hand protectively on her bump. She smiled. 'He or she—I hate saying *it*—just gave me a hefty kick. I think he or she is listening and giving his or her approval.'

Alex smiled too, his eyes lit with a warmth that thrilled her. 'I think the baby is telling me to take you home and love you and make a happy life together.'

'That baby has the right idea,' she said.

She swung herself out of bed so she could slide more comfortably into his arms. 'We're already married so I can't really ask you to marry me, but I think I will anyway. Alex, will you be my husband for real?'

'So long as you'll be my wife,' he said.

She laughed. 'I think we both agree on that. I love you, Mr Mikhalis.'

'I love you too, Mrs Mikhalis,' he said as he kissed her again, long and lovingly.

CHAPTER EIGHTEEN

One year later

DELL RELAXED BACK in the shade of the pavilion near the swimming pool and watched as her husband played with their daughter in the water. Litsa squealed in delight as Alex lifted her up in his arms and then dipped her into the water with a splash. 'We'll have her swimming before she's walking,' he called.

The baby gurgled her delight. At just six months old, she was nowhere near talking but she was very communicative, as she'd been in the womb. She and Alex had had endless fun making up meanings for her bump's kicks and wiggles.

Dell waved to her precious little lookalike. Litsa had been born with her mother's auburn hair and creamy skin but with brown eyes. People often remarked that she had the best of both her and Alex. Husband and wife would look at each other and smile. Alex had legally adopted Litsa. They would choose the right time to one day tell her about her biological father.

Alex need not have worried about bonding with the baby. As he'd promised, he'd been there at the birth and had adored his daughter at first sight. So had Dell. Motherhood was everything she had dreamed of. Even more as she was enjoying it buoyed with the love and support of the husband she grew to love more each day.

She and Alex had debated whether or not to move back to Sydney but had decided to stay in Greece, at least in the short term. Pevezzo Athina had been such a success that it was already completely booked out for the season and beyond. They still lived in the pavilion but Alex had started building them a magnificent new house out of sight of the resort but within sight of the little church where they'd married and Litsa had been christened. Her blog had taken a slight change in direction but had not lost her any readers—rather she had gained them.

The best news was that Alex's father, George, had gone into remission and was a devoted grandfather when he visited Greece, which he did more often. He and Eleni even talked of buying a house nearby when they retired and living between both countries.

Much to Dell's surprise her mother had become the most doting of grandmas—after she'd got over the hurt of being excluded from the wedding. When Dell had taken her into her confidence and explained why, her mother had forgiven her. She'd surprised Dell by telling her that she and her father had always disliked Neil but hadn't wanted to criticise their daughter's choice of husband. When they'd flown to Greece to meet their new son-in-law, her parents had given their full approval. Alex had taken to them too.

There was a friendly rivalry between her mother and Eleni over who would spend the most time in Greece with their granddaughter. When the grandmothers had met after Litsa's

birth, they'd realised they'd met each other before at a pharmaceutical conference and a genuine friendship had formed.

Who knew? Dell now mused. She would have
to figure out a time to tell both the grandmas
her news at the same time.

Alex gave Litsa a final plunge in the pool and
swung her up into his arms to a peal of baby
giggles. As her husband walked out of the pool,
his lean, powerful body glistening with water,
Dell felt the intense surge of love and desire she
always felt for him.

'Are you feeling okay?' he asked. 'Need more
dry crackers, more lemonade?'

'Ugh,' she said. 'No, thanks.'

No one had been more surprised than Dell
when she'd fallen pregnant. For so long she'd
thought herself the problem in her battles with
fertility. Turned out she'd been married to the
wrong man. Or that was what Alex said anyway.
She could only agree.

* * * * *

If you've enjoyed this book, look out for
THE BRIDESMAID'S BABY BUMP
by Kandy Shepherd. Available now!

If you want to treat yourself to another
second chance romance, look out for
A MARRIAGE WORTH SAVING
by Therese Beharrie.

MILLS & BOON®
Large Print – September 2017

The Sheikh's Bought Wife
Sharon Kendrick

The Innocent's Shameful Secret
Sara Craven

The Magnate's Tempestuous Marriage
Miranda Lee

The Forced Bride of Alazar
Kate Hewitt

Bound by the Sultan's Baby
Carol Marinelli

Blackmailed Down the Aisle
Louise Fuller

Di Marcello's Secret Son
Rachael Thomas

Conveniently Wed to the Greek
Kandy Shepherd

His Shy Cinderella
Kate Hardy

Falling for the Rebel Princess
Ellie Darkins

Claimed by the Wealthy Magnate
Nina Milne

MILLS & BOON®
Large Print – October 2017

Sold for the Greek's Heir
Lynne Graham

The Prince's Captive Virgin
Maisey Yates

The Secret Sanchez Heir
Cathy Williams

The Prince's Nine-Month Scandal
Caitlin Crews

Her Sinful Secret
Jane Porter

The Drakon Baby Bargain
Tara Pammi

Xenakis's Convenient Bride
Dani Collins

Her Pregnancy Bombshell
Liz Fielding

Married for His Secret Heir
Jennifer Faye

Behind the Billionaire's Guarded Heart
Leah Ashton

A Marriage Worth Saving
Therese Beharrie

0917 Rom LP

MILLS & BOON®

Why shop at millsandboon.co.uk?

Each year, thousands of romance readers find their perfect read at millsandboon.co.uk. That's because we're passionate about bringing you the very best romantic fiction. Here are some of the advantages of shopping at www.millsandboon.co.uk:

* **Get new books first**—you'll be able to buy your favourite books one month before they hit the shops

* **Get exclusive discounts**—you'll also be able to buy our specially created monthly collections, with up to 50% off the RRP

* **Find your favourite authors**—latest news, interviews and new releases for all your favourite authors and series on our website, plus ideas for what to try next

* **Join in**—once you've bought your favourite books, don't forget to register with us to rate, review and join in the discussions

Visit **www.millsandboon.co.uk**
for all this and more today!